THE WICKED REX OF THE WEST

ADVANCE PRAISE FOR
THE WICKED REX OF THE WEST

§ § §

"A journey so wild and unpredictable, it'll leave you reeling."
– Samantha Kolesnik, author of *True Crime*

"A mash-up that shouldn't work...but does! Nerdlo & Kappauff deliver a balls-to-the-wall reimagining that is compulsively entertaining!"
– Steve Stred, author of *Ritual*

"Daron and Ward's story is like a bit of.... Wait, I won't do that. It's a buffet of sarcasm, unlikeliness and balls-to-the-wall action I don't think you've ever encountered before. A fun read, definitely."
– John F.D. Taff, Multiple Bram Stoker Award nominee and author of *The Fearing*.

"You've heard the story from Dorothy, the Wicked Witch of the West, and Oz himself; but what about the dinosaurs? *The Wicked Rex of the West* is a wild, fun, and bloody ride through the land of Oz as created by the owners of Jurassic Park. With a dash of post-apocalypse and more than a fair share of adventure, you'll find yourself turning pages faster than a raptor running towards its prey."
– Sonora Taylor, award-winning author of *Little Paranoias: Stories* and *Seeing Things*.

"Oh, this is fun. A little like falling asleep under a tree, dreaming about being chased by tweakers, jumping in a dumpster that gets sucked up by a tornado that lands in Wonderland so you can ride on a T-Rex and save your new friends from The Wicked Bitch, kind of fun. This zany romp is bananas and I enjoyed the ride"

– Sadie Hartmann, *Mother Horror*

"A pop-culture fueled, wildly funny, zany-ass apocalyptic *Wizard of Oz* meets *Jurassic Park* love child of a book you never knew you needed. Daron and Ward have created a ridiculously fun romp with this one"

– Michael Patrick Hicks, author of *Friday Night Massacre*

"A gonzo tour-de-force."

– TC Parker, author of *Saltblood*

THE WICKED REX OF THE WEST

DARON KAPPAUFF
& WARD NERDLO

If you did not purchase this book, or receive a copy from the publisher, you are engaging in theft. Please don't. Thank you.

First Paperback Edition
Copyright © 2021 by Hold My Beer Publishing
Cover design by Edward Lorn
Interior design by Dullington Design Co.

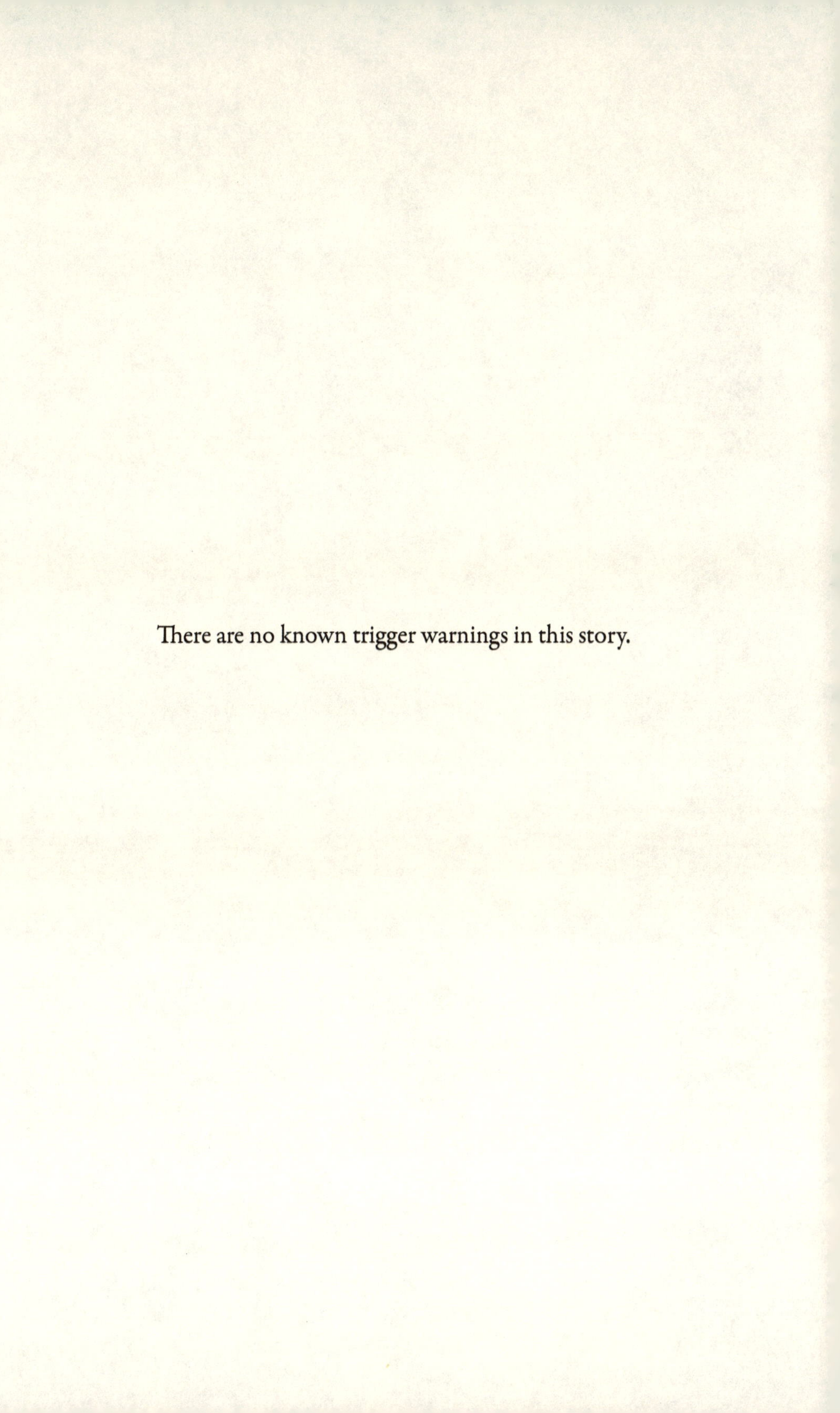

There are no known trigger warnings in this story.

This book is dedicated to the memory of Kevin Watkins (1975-2020). Because without his endless support and encouragement, it might not exist.
We miss you.

INTRODUCTION

by Laurel Hightower

You know that scene in *The Last Exorcism* when Cotton Marcus tells the film crew he's going to work his grandmother's banana bread recipe into his sermon? He does it successfully, the church raising hands over their heads and calling hallelujah, and Cotton gives this little grin to the camera. The book you're now holding is that same grin, delivered by Edward Lorn (writing as Ward Nerdlo) and Daron Kappauff after doing the impossible.

As is so often the case with works that fall into the "Laurel's Fault" subgenre, a Twitter conversation was the impetus for this mash-up. Back in early February 2020, I responded to a thread started by E asking about gimmicky book promos that get on your nerves. "Blurbs that use "tour de force" and descriptions that use shit like "Jurassic Park meets The Wizard of Oz..." was my response, and Twitter being Twitter, we quickly progressed to dinosaurs spiraling into twisters and armies of flying velociraptors. (Shout out to S.D. Vassallo for that particular gem.) Daron and E began a conversation behind the scenes and managed to build a world and outlined the thing while the rest of us were still giggling at E's proposed title: *The Wicked Rex of the West.*

Over the next days and weeks, we got regular updates that assured us a project that started as a joke was moving forward in an organized fashion. Two authors who barely knew each other threw themselves into an ambitious collaboration, and the result wasn't some *Epic Movie* phone-in where the elements are thrown in just for the ridiculousness of seeing them together, right before the entire cast breaks into a dance number because the writers have no idea what to do with them. Daron and E are writers first, and ridiculous second, so *Rex* was crafted with skill and care. They sent me the finished, edited project on January 2nd, and as I'm writing this it's February of 2021. In the space of a single year this off the wall project had been completed and polished from stem to stern. Color me impressed.

Even more so because of the way this book defied all my expectations, as I believe it will for all its readers. This is a skillful weaving of two storylines that were never meant to get within spitting distance of one another. Neither plot is reproduced here – you're not getting a regurgitation of *The Wizard of Oz* or *Jurassic Park.* Instead, Lorn and Kappauff built a separate world with nods to the source material. What results is a well-crafted, character driven action flick of an experience, with Easter-egg like inclusion of elements that are fun to discover, while quickly becoming their own thing. Dorothy, Toto, the Witch, Scarecrow, the Cowardly Lion and the Tin Man all make appearances, but as entirely new creations. A reader who had never experienced either movie or book could take *Rex* at face value, sit down and have themselves a hell of a fun ride.

Even more fun is the knowledge that there are more mashups in the works from this dynamic duo, with another favorite author adding her might. There's a lot to love about this whole situation – building friendships, stretching writing muscles, learning to do things as a writer that sound impossible. Twitter can certainly be the cesspool of doom scrolling and shouting into the void that we've all experienced from time to time. But to me, this is the real beauty of our online social connections, and the horror community as a whole. I love that folks can touch each other's lives in ways they never expected, that projects can be born and produced entirely from those kinds of connections. I'm proud of whatever small role I might have played in sending these two friends off on this journey, but I have a feeling they'd have found their way there, one way or another. Here's to more collaborations, more crazy ideas, and more connections. I'm raising a bourbon to you both.

February 24, 2021
Lexington, KY

CHAPTER 1

Dumpster Diving

Dot walked under the sepia sky of a suburban Kansas landscape. The air was haunted by the ghosts of drifting smoke as people burned leaves in their backyards. Fall had come to this section of the world, and there was a chill about things. Not cold but pleasantly cool. Tract houses scrolled past as if each had been installed on a treadmill set to a brisk walk. A T-Rex ran by, squealing gibberish to uncaring ears. It was probably just a tweaker in a dinosaur costume, but Dot fantasized that it was a real dinosaur, running through a world populated by anthropomorphic Jurassic-era creatures. *The Land Before Time* had been a childhood favorite of hers, and a much younger Dot had longed to run with Littlefoot and his crew.

*Ah, what dreams may come...*A smile crept across her face as the screeching king of the lizards faded into the distance. She was happy, happier than she'd been in years, because she'd finally gotten a job. The homestead would be saved. Or its death delayed. One or the other. At least, that was the hope. If that turned out not to be the case, Dot didn't know what they would do.

With the rise of industrialized farming came the collapse and bankruptcy of traditional farms. Huge conglomerates had bought up land and farmers alike, and people who once lived off the land had become cogs in a greater corporate wheel, one that ground self-esteem and churned out profits. Uncle Henrich blamed the popularity of veganism. The way he saw it, veganism had made automated farming a necessity because regular folks like him couldn't keep up with demand. Meat prices were down nearly everywhere, too, and you had to own a fishery if you wanted to make a profit in today's B-12-deficient society. Aunt Emily blamed society's lack of respect for hardworking folks. It was easy to ignore the little man when you buried him under corporate greed. Furthermore, no one cared about saving individually owned farms because they preferred the lower costs that massive companies provided. Dot blamed her aunt and uncle for not changing with the times, for being unable to adapt to the rise of organic living and the decreasing need for animal byproducts. Change was good. Change kept things interesting. Change was profitable.

The homestead had seen better days, days it would never see again. The electricity had been shut off going on three months now, and the propane tank drained since the previous Christmas. January and February had been a frozen hell. Numerous layers of quilts and comforters didn't do much when the blankets were freezing too. How Dot survived, much less how her aged aunt and uncle managed to, was beyond her capacity to figure out. Luckily there was well water to be had, because a water bill would only have served as toilet paper there at the end of the farm. Due to all of this, the three of them had moved into government housing located, according to Henrich, on the Wrong Side of the Goddamn Tracks: Bum Fuck Egypt.

Henrich had always had a mouth on him.

Now, every day brought with it the struggle to avoid being killed by some random white-trash meth-head looking to score twenty dollars by carving it out of your ass, or getting shot by the cops who arrived to apprehend said meth-head. Dot had a constant crick in her neck from continually looking over her shoulder. If you couldn't trust the civilian populace or the local authorities, who could you trust? Yourself, that's who. She supposed that was one plus to moving into the city; it had toughened her up far more than any country living had.

At the corner up ahead, on the opposite side of the road, stood a trio of wasted youths: all males in wife-beaters, each one's sallow complexion sallower than that of the guy to his left. They were a descending color palette, growing paler by the swatch. The closer Dot got to the group, the fewer teeth she saw, as if they were losing them in real time. Which reminded her of a joke.

What has three teeth and four boobs?

Nightshift at Waffle House.

Ba dum ts!

"Hey, Momma, what it do?" the palest one shouted. He grabbed his crotch, pinching his baggy jeans, which likely held nothing but fabric and air. His penis was likely an innie. Only tiny-dick assholes acted like this.

The middle whiteboy licked his lips. For the briefest second, Dot saw herself through his eyes: gone was the tired young woman, her long auburn hair tied up in a disheveled bun, her Sunday-best on display in the middle of the week; no, all this shit stain saw was a steak dinner, cooked medium rare, dripping juices. She shivered.

"We's talkin' to you, shawty," the darkest cracker of the bunch—which wasn't saying much, if she were honest; like calling a glass of water less wet than an ocean—hiked up his own sagging pants. Dot would have sworn before a jury of her peers she'd seen a camel's toe. This guy was probably nothing but nutsack too. Probably dribbled on his balls when he pissed.

Being a woman came with its perks: catcalls, periods, unequal pay, objectification, and the near-constant disrespect of the opposite sex. What a time to be alive.

Sarcasm aside, Dot tried not to focus on the bad, especially not now when her heart was full to bursting with pride at having just gained sustainable employment. So what if it was a cashier position at Queen Burger? Work was work. And any paycheck was better than staring at the unflinching zeroes of the family's joint bank account. When they'd had an account, anyway. The bank had finally closed it due to three-months of insufficient funds.

The tweaker in the middle said: "Got any fries with that furburger?"

"Sorry, guys, heading home. Talk tomorrow, okay? Thanks!" Dot sped up a bit. Just enough to show she was in a hurry, but not enough for it to seem like she was prey fleeing a group of predators, which was exactly what she was doing. She knew you should never run from a hungry animal, no matter how weak and docile it might seem. In fact, the hungry ones were the ones you had to worry about because they were desperate, and nothing's more dangerous than a desperate animal.

"But we wanna talk *now*!" called the palest tweaker as he stepped off the curb in her direction. They were across the street, but that single step off the sidewalk was too close, far too close, and Dot's fight or flight kicked in. Had she had time to think, she would've turned and stood up to them. That might've gotten her killed, of course, but more often than not, showing she wasn't scared worked a charm, especially with guys like these three.

This time, though, she ran.

The chase was on.

Dot never looked back. Not once. Uncle Henrich would've been proud of her for that alone. It had been one of his earliest lessons to her: "If you spot trouble, run and never look back." This of course went against the idea that she was always looking over her shoulder, but that was in search of trouble and not while fleeing it.

Besides, she could hear their hollow footfalls, as the emaciated feet inside their ratty sneakers slapped the pavement. She didn't have to turn around to tell they were gaining on her. Her mind was doing a perfect job of imagining the trio of tweakers closing the distance, step by step, inch by inch, until they would be upon her, ripping and tearing.

Uncle Henrich's *Wrong Side of the Goddamn Tracks* quote was literal: as in, a train track ran through the center of Nowheresville, Kansas, and this track did, in fact, separate the good neighborhood (the suburbs) from the bad neighborhood (the projects) in which Dot and her aunt and uncle lived. *The Wrong Side of the Goddamn Tracks* was mostly liquor stores with names like The E-Z Drunk and Liver Assassins, while the good side was mostly shit like Privates Grocery and Hobby Barn. Furthermore, there were far more churches located on *The Wrong Side of the Goddamn Tracks*, whereas religion was harder to come by on the good side—a drowning man will reach for a life preserver whether it exists or not. *The Right Side of the Goddamn Tracks* had its churches, sure, but they were few and far between, and big enough to host a stadium's worth of screaming Jesus fans, should the need arise. The churches on *The Wrong Side of the Goddamn Tracks* were smaller in size yet larger in number. You had your Pentecostals with their speaking in tongues, your Baptists with their hooting and hollering, and your Seventh Day Adventists with their services on Saturday because Sundays were sanctified. There was even a Catholic church, as well as a Synagogue and Mosque, although the latter was on the verge of moving out of town due to the constant harassment it had suffered.

Dot dashed across the tracks as storm clouds gathered ahead of her—a wall of darkness building at the end of the world like some great mythical beast of lore. The beast rolled closer, quicker now that Dot was running toward it. She smelled rain on the air, and something else. Something electrical. Ozone, maybe? Impending doom?

Best not to consider such things. Best to just keep running.

A grunt issued behind her and something grazed her back, like inexperienced fingertips down the skin of a lover. She heard the tweaker hit the ground and fancied the possibility that she'd heard a bony snap mixed in with the chaos of his tumble.

Good. I hope he broke his fucking neck.

And still, she never looked back.

She hooked right into the alley that ran behind The E-Z Drunk and the Wash Yo-Self laundromat. Instead of breaking Uncle Henrich's code and glancing over her shoulder, she homed in on the sounds of the remaining two tweakers' footsteps. They were farther away, around the corner she'd turned when entering the alley, and would be unable to see her, she judged, should she duck out of sight. Praying she was right, she dropped into the space between a dumpster and an abandoned grease trap left behind from a time when The E-Z Drunk had been a restaurant called Paco's Tacos. The smell back there was unbearable; something akin to rotten bananas and fresh-cut onions.

The wind whipped and howled, thankfully blowing some of the stench away from her, but it also covered the sounds of her pursuers' sneakers on the pavement. She strained to hear but couldn't discern running feet from the sounds of grit and trash slapping against the cinder block walls of The E-Z Drunk. Moreover, it seemed as if every machine inside Wash Yo-Self was running at the same time, further impeding her ability to hear the tweakers approaching.

All she could do was close her eyes and pray. She drew her knees to her chest, pressed her back into the filthy, possibly piss-soaked corner where the cinderblock wall met the dumpster, and asked God to prove his existence by carrying her away to safety.

Time passed. How much was anyone's guess.

Nothing happened.

And then...

A tongue.

On the knuckles of her right hand.

Someone was licking her.

She steeled herself, fully expecting to open her eyes and find a greasy-haired, sallow-faced tweaker treating the back of her hand like his favorite soft-serve flavor.

Her eyes damn near creaked as they opened.

It was a dog.

A Chihuahua, to be exact.

Dot loosed a pent-up breath in a shaky exhale. She scooped the doggo up under its forelegs and brought him to her chest. He smelled of corn chips and trash, although the latter was surely the smell of her surroundings and not the odor emanating from its hide. Said hide was oily and patchy, with sections of hairless skin the size of half-dollars here and there, as if something had taken small bites out of it. The poor guy was obviously suffering from mange, or some other skin disease, and Dot briefly considered whether she should be holding him at all. Could humans catch mange? She didn't think so. But perhaps mange was called something different when it hopped over to humans. Were psoriasis and eczema just human mange? Why was she thinking about this kinda shit when she was hiding from possible killers and rapists?

"What's your name?" she whispered to the dog, still aware that her tweaker pals could show up again at any moment.

Seven years ago, when she was but a twelve-year-old girl who aspired to one day be a veterinarian, Dot had ridden with Aunt Emily to the local vet for a day of volunteering. She'd assisted in several tasks that afternoon, one of which was chipping and tattooing animals so they might be easily found should they become lost or stolen. Every doggo got a chip inserted under the skin, then a small prison-green tattoo inside its ear. When she asked the vet if the tattoo hurt, the balding fat man had flashed her a yellow smile and said, "Life is pain, m'dear."

She never returned to that vet's practice, and even thinking about him now made her sick to her stomach. She'd ruminated on calling her local humane society to report him but decided against it. It would have been his word against hers, as was so often the case when a woman reported a man for anything.

She checked the chihuahua's ear and found not the simple green line denoting that he was chipped—she held the doggo aloft and found that *it* was indeed a *he*—but that his name was written there. One simple word suggesting frilly skirts and leggings:

Tutu.

"Tutu is an odd name for a doggo," she whispered.

"YAP!" Tutu proclaimed.

Dot grabbed Tutu's snout and squeezed his mouth closed. She released the pressure almost immediately, though, so as not to hurt the little guy.

"Sorry," she hissed.

Tutu's tongue lolled from the corner of his mouth as if to say, "All's good!".

That tongue...

Jesus, it was so long. Almost twice as long as his snout.

Was it called a snout? Dot truly didn't know. She thought maybe it was called a muzzle, but she also thought that a muzzle was something that went *over* a snout. Whatever. Did it really matter what word she used to describe it, in her own head?

"My, what a long tongue you have," Dot whispered. "You can probably taste yesterday with that thing."

"Yap," Tutu said, ever so softly.

"You're a smart boy, too, aren't you?"

Tutu panted in agreement.

"Are you lost?"

He cocked his head, as if to say, "What's a *lost*?"

"Do you have people?"

His head cocked in the other direction.

Dot sighed. "I wish you could talk to me."

"YAP!" This time, Dot jumped. Her head snapped back and gonged against the dumpster. The world around her tilted. She rubbed her throbbing skull as a dizzy spell threatened to bring on explosive emesis.

"You gotta stop that, Tutu," she groaned.

Tutu apologized with an inaudible "yap" and licked her cheek. All Dot could hear now was the howling of the wind. Pressure built in her ears, and an odd sensation of dislocation and drunkenness overcame her. She placed Tutu down at her feet and shimmied painfully up the rough cinder block wall until she was on her feet. Her knees almost unhinged but she remained upright. As her brain swirled, so did the air in the alley. The pounding pulse inside her skull sounded like distant tribal drums. Holding her aching head in her hands, she stumbled out from between the dumpster and the grease trap.

She looked left and found nothing but detritus twirling in the air, like massive dust motes in a ray of sunshine.

She glanced right and found her two tweaker pals stationed at the end of the alleyway, both their heads snapping back and forth, seeking their prey. Luckily, for now anyway, their backs were to her.

The wind churned and raged. Somewhere far away, a train could be heard, its rumbling engine chugging down the tracks toward them. If she could maybe make it to *The Good Side of the Goddamn Tracks* again, before the train arrived, she might put enough distance between herself and the angry tweakers. She might escape with little more than a sore noggin, and that would be just swell indeed.

She took a step backward and was suddenly sitting on her ass. Tutu leaped into her lap and pawed her chest. His rough tongue slapped at her face.

The noise of the approaching train grew to a growling crescendo.

Dot's twisted and tilted vision cleared. The tweakers had noticed her. They weren't coming for her. Not yet, anyway. They seemed to be looking... *through* her? Past her?

Dot went against Uncle Henrich's advice and glanced over her shoulder.

A sepia-toned twister was speeding down the alleyway toward her. Her basic survival instinct kicked in, sending her rolling between the dumpster and the grease trap once more. Impossibly, the twister raced *past* where she hid, heading directly for the tweakers standing at the alley's ingress. Dot heard their screams even above the howling tornado. She was aware that the twister should've snatched her up as it passed, but to say she wasn't in the clearest frame of mind would've been an understatement on a par with: outer space is on the big side.

Something vaguely tweaker-shaped shot into the sky like a rocket. The shape must've gone a hundred feet, at least, before it lost upward momentum and plummeted to earth. It splattered all over the ground, painting her red, like a monotone Jackson Pollock painting.

She tried not to look at the pile of smashed flesh and splintered bone directly in front of her. No way was she climbing over that mess of tweaker just to get sucked up by some picky twister. Also, there was no way she was climbing inside the grease trap and hiding in years-old lard and God only knew what else.

The dumpster was her only choice.

Somehow, she managed to get to her feet. Going was slow, but she made it. And as she did, the twister reappeared, sliding back into the alleyway with the remaining tweaker spinning inside like a discarded toy in a vacuum.

From within the tornado, the tweaker screamed: "I'm gonna get you, you bitch, and your fuckin' dog, too!"

The twister spat him out with such force that he was reduced to nothing but a crimson smear on the cinder block wall.

Without considering her lack of options another second, Dot threw open the lid of the dumpster and jumped in. She landed in a pile of what she hoped were wet trash bags with a grunt and a moan. She clawed and climbed, reaching for the dumpster lid. The twister was coming. If she didn't close the lid, she'd end up yet another red stain splashed about The E-Z Drunk's back alley. Her hair whipped wildly about her head until she finally snagged the lid and pulled it down.

Which was when she heard it.

"YAP! *YAPYAPYAP!*"

Tutu was jumping and scraping at the dumpster wall, begging to be saved. She threw the lid open once more and bent nearly in half, the cold, hard edge of the dumpster cutting into her gut, as she extended as far as she could without falling out.

Tutu was too far, and time was running short.

The twister tugged, beckoning her into its churning belly.

"JUMP!" she screamed, and Tutu jumped. Dot caught him and slung him into the softness of the piled trash beneath her. She snatched the lid at the exact moment the entire dumpster left the ground.

CHAPTER 2

Down the Rabbit Hole

The dumpster bounced through the night sky like a pinball ricocheting from bumper to bumper, climbing higher and moving farther into the funnel. Outside, the tornado chugged like a steam engine, the dumpster within twisting and rolling. Particulates plinked and thunked against the dumpster walls, causing the interior of the bin to thrum with cacophonous ringing. Inside, Dot had wedged herself across the elevator of terror, her feet pressed against the far wall, her hands against the one behind her head. Tutu had dug himself a tunnel in the trash, and Dot could feel the little scavenger somewhere near the small of her back. The dumpster upended and Dot drifted into the air before it righted itself and she plummeted once more into bagged refuse. That was close. Had the lid come open, she surely would've been sucked out into the storm. Which begged the question: what would happen when she landed?

I'm going to die. I'm going to die. I'm going to die.

The dumpster's lid flapped open and closed in the wind. Each time it raised, Dot sucked in a breath. She'd get a quick view of the swirling vortex outside, then pinch her eyes tight, not wanting to see oblivion as it approached. The final time the lid lifted, it revealed the night sky, clear and dark and full of stars.

Is that the eye of the storm?

Her stomach launched into her chest.

Freefall.

The metal dumpster pulled away as gravity reclaimed it as its own. Dot and the trash beneath her floated into the foul air. When her butt came away from the pile of trash, the lid flipped up. It remained at a ninety-degree angle as they dropped, flapping like a flag on a pirate ship. Pieces of trash leaped toward the stars, her shoes and socks with them. The blood-covered shoes had kept slipping against the slick metal walls, so she'd taken them off in hopes of getting better purchase with her bare feet.

Tutu yipped below her, the dog's rear legs rising into the air. Dot tried to grab him but missed by centimeters, so close that she felt the coarse prickle of his remaining hair on her fingertips. Tutu shot into the air, yapping. Dot was expelled too, before the trash bin slammed into the ground. Upon impact, a scream filled Dot's ears, then died as mysteriously as it had risen.

As she fell back in, Dot's forehead caught the rounded lip. The bin fell over, spilling trash and Dot onto the ground, like someone throwing out dirty dishwater. She rolled out atop the mountain of plastic bags, arms flopping lifelessly at her sides, and continued to tumble until she landed on verdant grass. Darkness consumed her.

§ § §

"Is she alive?"

"There's a lot of blood."

The voices faded in and out between the thudding of her heart, the blood pounding in Dot's ears, and the pain radiating across her forehead. The voices belonged to a young man and woman hovering above her. They spoke in hushed voices as one of them kept pacing past her head. She willed her eyes to focus, but the figures remained blurry shadows against starry night.

Dot was alive. But how she'd survived both the tornado and the fall was a complete fucking mystery. Why she wasn't smeared all over creation was beyond logic. The tweakers certainly hadn't been so lucky. She watched their deaths replay on a loop in her mind: the two of them exploding in the alley, their broken bodies splattering her like bird shit on a windshield. Reaching for her brow, she felt the golf-ball-sized lump and winced, teeth gritted against the pain. Touching it felt as if someone was stabbing her with an ice pick.

"Looks like she's coming to," the young woman said.

"What about the other one?"

Other one?

She'd been alone in the dumpster, except for Tutu, of course, and there was no way the poor little doggo had survived that fall. Her heart sank. It hadn't occurred to her that if *she* had survived, perhaps Tutu had too. Anyway, the young man hadn't said, *What about the dog*? He'd said, *What about the other one?*, implying another person. Maybe someone near the impact site?

"Don't think so. This thing weighs a ton," the young woman said. "She was crushed. Probably dead in an instant."

The scream...

At first, Dot had thought it'd come from her. But it couldn't have. She hadn't had the breath to scream as she'd fallen back to earth. Her air had been stolen by the sudden descent. Which left only one other possibility.

There'd been someone else at the crash site.

Oh God. Dot had killed someone. *Oh God.* But it wasn't her fault. *Right?* It's not like she'd intended to crush anyone with a goddamn dumpster. She hadn't been driving the damn thing, for fuck's sake. Plus, how do you not see a giant metal dumpster falling out of the sky? Yeah, just stand there like the blond chick in *Prometheus* and be smooshed by the easily avoidable falling object.

It's not my fault. No fucking way am I gonna be blamed for this.

Dot rubbed her eyes, trying to clear them, desperate to see what she'd done, while at the same time terrified of the looming evidence that she'd killed someone. She wasn't a murderer. She couldn't go to jail. Aunt Emily and Uncle Henrich would lose what little they had left without her income. She needed to work, to make money to help support her family. But how could she do that if she spent the rest of her life in prison, trying to avoid being assaulted by rape-y guards and even rapier convicts?

Taking a deep breath, she tamped down her anxiety. *No point in frettin' over things that haven't happened yet.* That's what her aunt had always said. Seemed like sage advice at that the moment. Dot needed to deal with what was in front of her, here and now; figure out what happened, and fabricate a story to explain her innocence. But she was no fool. The best-case scenario here would be a manslaughter charge; she was certain of it.

Her head was still spinning when the figures took shape. They were younger than she'd imagined––older teenagers, young twentysomethings at the most. Definitely siblings; possibly twins. Each had the same brown hair, green eyes, small nose, and high cheekbone structure. It looked like neither of them had showered in weeks, and holes and long tears peppered their clothes like buckshot.

Do they shop exclusively at thrift stores? Are they homeless?

The notion didn't surprise her, as much as she wished it did. They'd obviously had a hard life, living on the streets. But Dot knew she shouldn't be so judgmental. Her existence in the projects wasn't much better than a life bumming on the streets. Young people deserved better. Everyone did.

The dumpster laid on its side next to them, blood saturating the grass below and around it. A pair of thin legs, nearly severed below the knees, protruded from underneath. The bare legs were covered in blood and dirt––the blood fresh and wet, the dirt old and caked on. A pair of green flats made from some kind of reptile covered her feet. Their scales sparkled in the moonlight.

She *had* killed someone. The anxiousness clawed its way back up her throat, a spray of bile trailing behind. The noxious sick seared her esophagus like scalding soup traveling the wrong direction. Leaning to the side, Dot gagged, spewing her Queen Burger value meal into the pool of blood inches from her hand.

Oh, that's fuckin' gross.

She wiped vomit from her lips with the back of one hand.

"You alright?" the young man said as he extended a hand to help Dot to her feet.

"Other than my head, yeah." She touched her welt again and cringed at the jolt of pain that surged across her forehead. Two head injuries—one on the back of her skull, the other on the front—in less than an hour. Good chance she had a concussion. Maybe even slight brain damage. If she had done irreparable harm to her cognitive functions, would she even be able to tell?

Can this night get any better?

"What's your name?" the young man said.

"Dot." She crinkled her toes in the grass and looked herself over. She didn't seem to have any other injuries, although she did hurt all over. She'd need x-rays and rest, though, for sure.

"That's an interesting name." The young woman looked Dot up and down. "Is it short for anything?"

"Nope."

"I'm Victor Munch," the young man said. "And this is my sister, Victoria."

Victoria gave a little curtsey. She wasn't wearing a dress, so she grabbed the pockets of her jeans, crossed her legs, and bowed. She was cute, even given her current state of uncleanliness.

"Victor and Victoria, huh?" Dot said. "Adorable."

Disgusting, actually.

Victoria peered into the dumpster. "Were you in this thing when it landed?"

"Don't judge. I usually travel with a bit more style." Dot smirked. Not true, but they didn't need to know that. They also didn't need to know she couldn't even afford her own beater. Or that the only transportation her family owned was a rusted-out farm truck that had been sitting on E since time immemorial, or so it seemed.

The joke went over both teens' heads.

Victor nodded at the dead woman's legs. "You should probably take her shoes."

"Gross. I'm not wearing a dead person's shoes." Dot shuddered. "Plus, they're hideous."

"You can't walk around out here barefoot," Victoria said.

"Why not? It's just grass."

"Because if one of *them* shows up, and we have to run..." Victoria glanced around the empty clearing.

Dot hadn't taken in her surroundings, so she spared a minute to evaluate them. Luckily, the moon was bright enough to aid her investigation. She seemed to be in the middle of a rectangular meadow framed by trees on all sides. It looked like the future home of a stadium, or something like it, as if the land had been cleared for a super-sized building but the funding had fallen through before construction began.

As she continued to examine the area, she asked, "One of what?"

Victor and Victoria grimaced. Whatever it was, they didn't want to say.

"Just take the shoes," Victor said. "Please."

Rolling her eyes, Dot approached the dumpster and the shoes in question. She bent over, positioning herself on either side the corpse's legs, and retrieved the ugly footwear. She slipped them on. The scales weren't just decoration; they felt real.

Dot shrugged. "They're actually kinda comfortable." Scanning the trees around them, she added, "Where are we anyway?"

Her final assessment of the area was: trees and grass as far as the eye could see, a star-filled sky, no train tracks––good- or wrong-sided; no subsidized housing or churches, no abandoned businesses… no buildings of any kind, actually. The overwhelming presence of nature struck Dot as odd. She hadn't seen more than a handful of trees in months. Not since they'd been forced to move off the homestead. There weren't any parks this big anywhere near the projects. Where had the tornado taken her?

Something chirped on the far side of the dumpster.

No; it didn't chirp. It shrieked: high-pitched and shrill.

Dot and the twins froze. Victor positioned himself in front of his sister as the screech came again.

"The hell is that?" Dot's muscles tightened.

Fear filled the twin's faces. They recognized the sound. Was this the *them* they'd mentioned?

A squat creature rounded the dumpster; considered the three of them, then shrieked once more. Not even two-feet tall and covered in feathers, the winged beast looked like a turkey, but with a tail spanning three feet and a long snout––this creature definitely had a snout. It walked on two hind legs, a sickle-like talon rising from the center of each foot.

"Raptor!" Victoria screamed, and made herself as small as possible behind her brother, her head peeking around his arm. She was trembling something awful.

"What did you call it?" Dot glanced at the twins, then back at the turkey-thing. It would've been cute if not for the rows of razor-sharp teeth filling its mouth.

"It's a Velociraptor," Victor said. "We need to get on top of the dumpster, or up a tree. Somewhere it can't follow. Now!"

The twins sidestepped toward the upturned bin, their eyes wide.

Dot frowned and shook her head. "It's just some kind of bird."

"It's not a bird," Victoria said.

"And they hunt in packs," Victor added. "This is probably a scout."

Dot huffed. *This* was not a Velociraptor. She'd seen *Jurassic Park*—even the shitty reboots with the cute guy from *Parks and Recreation*. Raptors stood taller than humans and had scales, not feathers. She squatted and motioned the creature towards her. She didn't know why, but she felt a strange kinship with the odd-looking bird. Like they were connected.

"The hell are you doing?" Victor hissed. The siblings had reached the dumpster; Victor had his hands on Victoria's waist, hefting her up. "It's going to rip your throat out."

Dot sighed. Holding out her hand, she called the thing to her. It approached. Slowly. Like a curious dog investigating an unknown treat. When it was a few feet away, Dot could see the name *Tutu* tattooed on the creature's head, behind its right eye. The area had been shaved—plucked?— and the full moon provided more than enough light to see by.

What?

It couldn't be. The implication seemed impossible. But the closer the chihuahua-sarus got, the quicker the impossible transformed into the irrefutable. The turkey-thing was the dog she'd found in the alley.

How the fuck?

Tutu waddled over, neck extended, and sniffed Dot's hand. He lingered a moment, confirming his companion's scent, then curled up between Dot's legs and preened. Purring, Tutu leaned into Dot's hand as she ran it across his head, neck, and back. The feathers were smooth, as if freshly oiled, and oddly cold to the touch. Tutu nuzzled Dot's cheek with his own, a low reed-like whistle emanating from the back of his throat.

Slack-jawed, the twins gawked at the spectacle.

§ § §

"Let me get this straight." Hands planted on her hips, Dot stood in front of the dumpster the twins were perched on top of. Tutu sat in the grass next to her. "You're saying every dog on the planet somehow transformed into a dinosaur, overnight, and wiped out ninety-five percent of humanity?"

"Not somehow," Victoria said. "*Magic.*"

"Right...magic." Dot clucked her tongue and strolled across the clearing to a nearby tree. "Witches," she added in mock fascination.

Tutu raised off his haunches, eyeing the siblings, a small snarl climbing his throat.

"One of which was crushed by my flying dumpster." *Still not my fault, by the way.* "That about sum it up?"

Victoria glanced at the legs jutting from beneath the trash bin. "Pretty much."

"*And,* to top it off, this *magical night of death and destruction* occurred over a year ago, and I somehow missed it? Do you know how ridiculous that sounds?"

This had to be a dream. Or maybe she was dying? Maybe she'd hit her head when she'd crashed, cracked her skull open, and this was the crazy shit her scrambled brain cooked up as it slowly ticked toward death like a cooling engine.

Awesome...

"Question is," Victor said, "where have you been that you didn't know any of this? In a coma?"

"Think I'm in a coma now," Dot murmured. She strolled back to Tutu's side and petted his head.

Victor got on his knees and lowered a leg down off the dumpster. Tutu was under him in a second, snapping at his foot and barking––or whatever constituted barking for a dino-doggo. The young man scrambled up the dumpster and into his sister's arms. Panting, he glared at Tutu, shooing him with limp hands.

"Tutu, sit," Dot said, and the raptor sat.

"How did you...?" Victoria said.

Dot was all shoulders.

Tutu glanced at Dot then pranced back to her side.

"Whatever," Victor said. "We can figure all this out once we get indoors. We've been out in the open too long."

Dot snickered. "Worried about being eaten by a T-Rex?"

"Yeah," Victoria said.

"Each of the sisters has a pet tyrannosaurus." Victor's eyes dropped to the dead woman—the supposed witch. "This one's is probably looking for its master as we speak."

Dot huffed. "Right. Sure. Why not?"

The ground shook and a low growl echoed across the night; a tremor so strong, Dot's teeth chattered. A flock of shadowy figures exploded from the canopy of trees in the distance, filling the sky with darting specks of black, zipping across the face of the moon. Dot considered Tutu. He'd been a chihuahua before this crazy nightmare began. The thing stalking the shadows had probably been a pit bull.

"Holy shit," Dot said. "You weren't kidding."

Shaking in her brother's arms, Victoria's gaze bounced from tree to tree.

"We need to get out of here," Victor said. "It's close."

"Yeah. Okay," Dot said.

"What about..." Victoria's eyes fell to the dinosaur at Dot's feet. "*That*?"

"What, Tutu? He's harmless." Dot knelt and scratched both sides of the raptor's head. "Aren't you, boy?"

Tutu barked.

"See?" Dot said. "Now, where're we off to?"

The twins climbed down, eyes locked on the raptor. Tutu grumbled and whined but didn't leave Dot's side.

"We need to get out of the park and down to Yellow Road," Victor said. "That's where the base is."

Brow furrowed, Dot squinted at them. "Base? You the resistance or some shit?"

"Yeah." Victor took his sister's hand and ran for the exit.

CHAPTER 3

Welcome to...What?

The exit wasn't what Dot was expecting. She'd expected a door, an archway; hell, even a glowing EXIT sign above a turnstile. Anything other than a giant hole in what seemed to be a massive, electrified fence. Having grown up on a farm, Dot was well aware of what a zap-fence looked like, and this one was surely in the same category: large conical transformers atop sturdy steel poles; thin wire threaded intricately through vertical bars; a generator box nearby, nothing more than a four-foot cube cloaked in shadow at the edge of her vision.

Rent steel jutted around the perimeter of the "exit" like teeth in a monster's mouth. Wires dangled here and there, wires that Dot assumed had once spat and sparked while the fence had been powered on. Now the fence was obviously powered down, the wires dead. She wondered if there was power to any part of the park. Surely there had to be, right? No way were these people living in the dark. Then again, if what the twins said was true, that the world had ended when beloved pets turned to ravenous dinosaurs, then was a community living in darkness that big of a leap? Probably not.

"What did this?" Dot asked, her voice barely above a whisper.

Victor said, "That witch you crushed with your trash can—"

"Little more than a trash can, there, Vic," Victoria cut in.

"—her Rex did this. Leo had the grid powered down for maintenance one night. Crew came out to fix a faulty connection and got ambushed. The Rex ate all four of them, then tore hell out of this section of the fence. The barriers to the North, South, and West are all intact, though, so we're lucky we only have to watch this exit. Victoria and I were doing our mandatory rounds of the breech when we saw you come down. You know the rest."

"Jesus," Dot breathed. "And all this was put up by who, the last five percent of humanity?"

Victoria laughed. "That last five percent couldn't have tied their shoes properly in the aftermath of the witches' spell. No, this place was a zoo, back in the day. Dinos came because it was a great food source. All these tasty beasties sitting around, all caged up. It was like a buffet in a prison. Dinos ate all the animals. Cleared them out completely. And we moved in. With us here, the dinos returned. *It's the circle of life!*" Victoria sang the last bit in an ear-murdering impersonation of Elton John.

"Where do we go now?" Dot asked.

"We follow the road to the base. Won't be far. And now that we're through the exit, we only need to watch behind us. Everything else is secure," Victor assured her.

"Can't it get through into this section?" Dot asked.

"Yup," Victoria chirped.

"What do we do if that happens?"

Victor gave her a small, flat smile. "We run."

"Wonderful."

Up ahead, on either side of the black asphalt the twins called Yellow Road, the way was dotted with sparse ornamental streetlights: pale white globes mounted on poles shaped like ten-foot-tall vases. The lamps painted the way with their ghostly light, giving off an almost misty, streets-of-London vibe. The road beneath their feet was cobblestone, with flecks of yellow paint in places. Time and overuse had worn through most of the paint, so there wasn't much more than a speckling here and there, but still enough to show what once had been.

The three of them moved at a brisk pace, their shoes quietly slapping the road, while Tutu took the rear, claws clicking on stone, his little feathered head flicking this way and that at every miniscule sound the surrounding woods made. They walked for an indeterminate amount of time before a voice boomed, seemingly from all around them:

"Who's there?"

"What the—" Dot started.

"It's Victor and Victoria!" Victor called. "We found another survivor!"

The world flashed a brilliant white. Dot smashed her lids closed against the painful glare. Her vision went red as the intense light bled through her eyelids.

"Chill with the spotlights, Crow!" Victoria hollered.

"She safe?" the voice asked. The boom was gone, the theatrical tone now nothing more than a tinny voice through a loudspeaker.

"She doesn't have scales, does she?" Victor said.

"You know that don't mean shit!"

Victor called back, "Crow, calm your tits, man. Her name's Dot, and she has a—"

"DINO!" the voice named Crow boomed.

"Shit," Victor said as the gunfire began.

Dot, her eyes still closed, bright white orbs dancing across the inside of her lids as if someone were playing Pong on a dying television, was yanked to the side. She stumbled and hit the ground. She could hear Tutu's yaps, and the click of his claws on the asphalt as he scampered away from the bullets.

"STOP!" she cried. "HE'S WITH US!"

The gunfire continued.

Dot forced her eyes open. Her vision blurred, tilted, and then corrected in time to see Tutu dive between the bars of the dead fence and vanish into the tree line across the road.

"Fuck!" Crow growled through the loudspeaker. "The little fucker is *fast*!"

"He's with me, you asshole!" Dot raged.

"With you?" Crow's disembodied voice floated on the air. "What the hell are you talking about?"

"It's with her. She can talk to it. It listens to her." Victor said as he picked himself up from the grass and dusted off his pants.

"Nonsense."

This Crow guy was going to be a handful, Dot just knew it.

"It's true, you nimwit. We saw it ourselves."

"The hell you preach," Crow said.

Victoria rolled her eyes. "If he only had a brain…"

A light clicked on a little farther ahead, illuminating a tree stand in the middle of the road that stood about fifty feet from Dot's current position. A tall, thin figure climbed down from the blind with gangly, clumsy movements. When the he reached the ground, he walked—if such a stuttering, wobbly gait could be called walking—toward the group, his face drifting in and out of shadow as he passed from one streetlight to the other. He stopped a few feet away, under one of the ornamental lights, and gave Dot a hideous frown. She hated to think of the guy as Freakshow material, but the thought did cross her mind. She could see his deformed mug on posters with callsigns like "Come see the Quilted Man and watch him piece himself back together!"

"The fuck happened to your face?" Dot blurted. Not her best moment, for sure.

"A dinosaur, like the one travelling with you, little lady. Cut me up real good." Crow traced the fleshy seams of his face, where someone had tried their best to stretch skin into places it should've been but wasn't. The grafts weren't anything you'd expect from a proper surgeon, and Dot was shocked the man was standing at all. "I got the fucker in the end, though. Blew his brains out his tail, I did."

Crow unshouldered a rifle to use as a cane, of sorts, the barrel digging into the toe of his left boot. Dot didn't know a thing about gun safety, but she was damn sure such a pose wasn't in the best interest of his little piggies.

Dot shoved herself to her feet. "You ran my dog off."

"I dint see no dog, little lady."

"Stop calling me that. My name's Dot."

"Dot it is then. Crow. Scar Crow, for obvious reasons." He held out a hand, which Dot ignored.

Huh. With the lines on his face, the scars, the fact that it kinda looks like he's wearing a burlap sack...Does he realize how close his name is to—

He put away his proffered hand. "And, yes, the name is a pun. People are assholes, but if the shoe fits..." Crow shrugged.

"And you...what? Sit up in your stand, shooting at innocent animals for fun?" Dot said.

"Dint look innocent to me. No dinosaur's innocent. They're all walking, talking stomachs with teeth. They'd eat ya soon as look at ya."

"Tutu isn't like that," Dot said.

"Sure thing. Last time I took someone's word for how docile their pet was, I was prying a Pomeranian off my leg with a pair of pliers for the better part of an hour. That was back before the Change, though." Crow sniffed and adjusted his belt.

"Real good with animals, this one." Dot huffed a mirthless laugh.

"We ain't talkin' just any animals, missy. We're talking killing machines. Perfect killing machines. Don't get it twisted. Would you have a pet shark? How 'bout a Grizzly? Hell, maybe you're one of them what thinks all animals is kind and sacred and we humans are the problem. I wouldn't doubt it. It was your kind screwed up the world long before the Change."

Dot let the jackass finish his tirade before she said, "Call me *missy* or *little lady* one more time and I'mma shove that rifle so far up your Hershey Highway you'll be picking lead out of your nose until Christmas, you dig?"

Crow barked laughter. "Hey, you might not be so bad after all!"

He slapped her on the shoulder.

She kneed him in the balls.

"Fuhg," blasted from Crow's mouth on a rush of air that smelled heavily of coffee, cigarettes, and, horrendously, fresh garlic.

Must be a joy to kiss. The tone of Dot's thoughts was so smug even she hated the sound of it.

The lanky man dropped to his knees, clutching his crotch, a sound issuing from his pursed lips like steam through a teakettle's spout. He rolled limply onto his side, where he stayed for a while, lamenting the unfairness of it all.

"Crow! Crow, come in!" This new voice was high-pitched, male, excited.

Victor snatched a small black square from Crow's shoulder and raised it to his face.

"This is Vic. Crow's...um...seeing about something important. What's going on?"

"Vic? Vic! Jesus buttfucking Christ, am I glad you're okay. Search team saw something fall from the sky at your last known location. Was worried the East's Rex had got you before we got it!"

"Wait...*what*? What do you mean *before you got it*?"

"We got her Rex, Vic! We caught the fuckin' thing. Took two teams. One to bait, one to trap, but we got the fucker!"

Victor met Dot's questioning eyes. "Well, this is interesting."

Victoria grabbed the Walkie Talkie from her brother. "Base, this is Victoria, how long ago did this happen?"

"Shortly before the gunfire at Crow's location."

Victoria addressed Victor: "So not long ago."

"Doesn't sound like it," Victor agreed.

"Fuhg," Crow groaned.

"They caught a Rex? The one that was after us?" Dot asked.

Victor nodded. "Sounds like that's the case, yeah."

"Hot damn!" Victoria shouted.

"Fuhg."

"Walk it off, little man," Dot said with a grin.

"Fuhg...you," Crow breathed.

Victor laughed. "I wouldn't piss her off anymore, Crow. Little lady has a mean kick."

"Watch it, Vic," Dot warned.

Victor, still laughing, raised both hands in a placating gesture. "I'm watchin', I'm watchin.'"

"Let's go. I gotta see this!" Victoria grabbed Crow's hand and yanked him to his feet.

"What about Tutu?" Dot asked.

"Have you tried calling him?" Victor asked.

"Oh." Dot hadn't even considered it. "Not yet. Lemme try." She cupped her hands around her mouth and shouted, "Tutu! Tutu, come, boy!"

The turkey-sized raptor scampered gleefully from the tree line, as if Dot had just opened a can of fresh dog food, and took his place by her side. She bent down to assess him. She ran her hands over his head, neck, torso, wings, and legs. The tiny dino didn't seem to be injured. Lucky little devil had dodged death twice so far today: a dumpster ride from hell, followed closely by some random stranger emptying a clip in his general direction. What a world, what a world.

"Keep that thing away from me," Crow growled.

"He's not who you have to worry about," Dot warned.

"Noted." Crow cleared his throat. "Can we go now?"

"Lead the way," Dot said, and the group resumed their trek.

§ § §

Ever since the family had run out of money to put a few gallons in the pickup's tank, Dot had done more than her fair share of walking. Because of this, she was able to count her steps and do some simple math to calculate the distance the group of five had travelled. In little over half a mile, they came to a solid concrete wall that ran off to the right and left, into the tree line. The wall was a good fifty feet tall, at least ten feet taller than the electrified fence they'd passed through earlier. While the wall itself was concrete, the massive double doors were made of wood, or perhaps something molded and grained to look like wood. She couldn't tell. Someone had slapped black paint over a sign on the right. On the left door, someone had spray-painted two words that both confused and offended her:

"Welcome to...*Homo Park*," Victor said with a flourish of his hands.

Dot said, "*Homo* Park? Why—"

Victoria cut her off. "It's short for *homosapien*. The men here think it's funny. Dudes being dudes. Locker-room talk, I've heard it called."

Dot rolled her eyes.

"Shall we?" Victor had moved off to the side, past the larger doors, to a smaller door that looked like it was attached to something akin to a ticket booth. "We don't open the big doors. We *never* open the big doors. That way, no one can forget to close them. Never open. Always safe. *Entrée*." Victor wrenched open the door, bowed, and swept his arm toward the lighted interior.

"Somebody wanna tell him that's not what *entrée* means?" Dot whispered.

"I reckon it means, like, food, or something, right?" Crow said, his face broadcasting loudly how unsure he truly was. Then again, given the state of his face, he could be cheesing like a fool and no one would be the wiser.

"And they say you're brainless. Good job, man." Victoria gave Crow a light pat on the shoulder as she passed him on her way inside.

Crow frowned. "Wait...huh? Who says I'm brainless?"

Victoria grinned over her shoulder. "*They* do."

"Buncha assholes," Crow said, as he followed Victoria into the base.

Dot, shaking her head, went next, Tutu close by her side.

CHAPTER 4

Get away from her, you bitch!

On the other side of the park's entrance, past a series of turnstiles, sat a massive quadrangle that sprawled out for fifty yards. A pair of buildings jutted into the quad on either side. One of the windows was shattered––only a few jagged reminders of its existence remained—and one was missing entirely. Inside of each window, numerous animal action figures and moldy plushies sat discarded, some on their sides, others laying in pools of shattered glass. A faded painting of a chubby blue giraffe with a round nose and big, happy eyes covered the door leading into one of the buildings. Dot thought the character would've been on the verge of a copyright infringement lawsuit from a particular toy seller had, you know... the world not ended. There was no door on the other building, so Dot could see inside unimpeded, and found mostly empty clothes racks and empty shelves.

Gift shops?

A series of work lights had been set up to form a makeshift pathway leading from the entrance to a cement walkway bisecting the quad. Along both sides of the pathway sat several permanent booths with moldering signage and peeling paint. One such establishment offered "The best pretzels money can buy!" while another boasted "The coldest drinks in the tri-county area!" Dot doubted the veracity of both statements. Another stand had been set up a little farther up to sell more of the plushies and plastic animal toys. These items had likely been the zoo's number one source of income––the way movie theaters didn't make much off admission, but killed with concessions. The lights continued down the right side of the walk, branching off into individual paths that led to the animal exhibits. Another pathway of light ran away from the original path until it disappeared behind a large stone outcropping that rose ten feet from the ground. Past the lights there was darkness, pure and primal and oppressive.

Dot glanced skyward. The night was clear, stars twinkling in their assigned locations, but something about those locations seemed off. Dot didn't recognize any of the constellations. It was like someone had poured paint over a perfect picture and then swung a brush at the canvas, splattering the image with little white blobs.

"The hell?" Dot said, her mouth agape.

Crow looked to the sky as well. He glanced at Dot, then back up. "Ain't you ever seen stars before?" he said, still peering into the night.

"Not these stars."

Shaking his head, Crow huffed and started down the path. "A star's a star, Miss Dot. Seen one, seen all twenty."

"Twenty?" Vic said, following the wobbly sharpshooter. "Jesus, Crow, you really are an idiot."

"What's wrong?" Victoria asked Dot, her eyebrows knitted together.

"Huh? Oh." *Oh is right. How do you explain to someone that you think the universe is out of alignment?* "It's nothing," Dot continued. "Just feeling a little dizzy. Probably just the rollercoaster ride that brought me here catching up to me. I'll be fine."

Dot smiled as Victoria raised her eyes to the stars. After a moment, the young woman huffed, shrugged, then started after her brother and Crow. Stifling a laugh, Dot followed, still gazing, still hoping to find something familiar. Her turkey-looking dinosaur-dog trailed behind. Tutu had been quiet since rejoining the party, after Crow had shot at him, and now the tiny creature seemed to be just as curious about his surroundings as Dot was. Could he have been thinking the same thing? That they weren't in Kansas anymore?

As they rounded the light that constituted the walkway's corner, the low roar of a great beast stopped the group in their tracks. Dot's blood ran cold, and her skin turned to gooseflesh. The creature was close. Real close.

"Was that..." Dot searched the darkness.

Up ahead, on the left.

"It's the Rex!" Vic slapped Crow on the shoulder and sped off. "Come on!"

The roar came again, but this time the earth shook with its ferocity. The shouting came next. A bunch of dudes yelling something incomprehensible at the top of their lungs. Then, the screaming began. Bloodcurdling and high pitched––the sound of someone's life being ripped away in the most painful manner possible.

That can't be good.

Dot chased after the others. They veered left off the walkway and into the grass. After a few strides, she noticed a metal railing rising from the ground a couple yards ahead, the legs bolted to a cement wall protruding two feet up from the earth. Vic was first to mount the low wall, hitting the railing with such speed that he nearly flipped over it. Victoria arrived next. She'd overtaken Crow, who could barely walk, let alone run, and took the position to Vic's right. Dot held back, allowing Crow to reach the security railing ahead of her. If there was one thing she'd learned about trouble, it was that a wise Samaritan is slow to react, lest she become a victim as well.

Climbing up next to Victoria, with Tutu at her side, Dot gasped as she peered over the railing.

The wall overlooked a pit. A habitat. Probably the zoo's big-cat exhibit—the pumas at the one back home were Dot's favorite. A handful more work lights illuminated the area, revealing the horrible scene below. Two men stood on each side of the Rex, holding metal wires that were wrapped around the creature's neck. They were attempting to secure the wires to a pair of large metal rings that had been bolted to two small cement slabs in the ground.

The Rex, however, wasn't having it. It swung its head back and forth, lifting the men off their feet with each pull. The owner of the aforementioned screams was pinned at the waist in the monster's mouth. Blood sprayed in sputtering gouts as the giant lizard thrashed back and forth. The man's screams were constant now, his arms and legs flailing out either side of the Rex's mouth.

"Holy shit!" Vic said. "Is that Larry?"

"O...M...G." The letters trickled from Victoria's mouth so slowly she could have added another word or two between each one.

As horrendous as the scene was near the Rex's mouth, Dot couldn't peel her eyes away from its back end. Some kind of machine held the dino's left leg and tail, preventing it from stomping on the four men in front of it.

No. Not a machine. It was a huge metal suit, piloted by a man standing at its center. It looked like the loader the chick from *Aliens* used to fight the queen bitch at the end of the movie, only this one was gunmetal gray rather than yellow. Metal plates had been welded to the front of the legs and around the sides of its torso, and the cockpit was encased in plexiglass, giving the thing an armored appearance.

What the actual fuck?

Dot shook her head. She closed her eyes and then opened them again. She was certain nothing like this armor existed in the real world. Not in her real world, anyway. When she opened her eyes, the mechanical man remained.

Where the fuck am I? This cannot be real.

Tutu had stuck his head over the side, below the railing, and was yipping at the much larger dinosaur. Napoleon syndrome.

"Guys?" Dot said, tapping Victoria's arm. "What the hell is——"

Larry's screams crescendoed, causing all four spectators to choke on a breath. The muscles in the Rex's jaw tightened, and the terrible lizard clamped down with all its might. Blood exploded out of its mouth as Larry was cut in three, silencing his screams. His upper and lower half fell away, a trail of bloody intestines flapping in the wind. The Rex retained the man's midsection, chomped it into small bits, raised its head, and swallowed.

The beast reared back, lifting all four men off the ground, then scooped its head down, hooked towards the sky, and roared. Its breath tussled Dot's hair, the rank smell turning her stomach; it reeked of death, like a skunk that had sprayed before being disemboweled and left to rot in the hot sun.

"Get 'em, Foil!" Crow said, his eyes fixed on the man piloting the mech.

"The fuck you think I'm doing, dumbass?" the man Crow referred to as Foil said. A piston hissed as the power suit stepped back, dragging the dinosaur towards it. It looked like the pilot was trying to flip the beast onto its side.

Tutu yipped again, this time at the mechanical suit.

"Tutu, hush." Dot glared at the little dino.

The turkeysaraus did as instructed; and even went a step further and sat at Dot's feet.

That's so strange.

The Rex spun at the armored man and roared, but with its leg and tail still restrained, it failed to even get close. It did, however, notice that the two men who were previously standing on its left side were now directly below. It lunged at the men, jaws snapping as it closed on them. Both men yelped and leapt away as the creature's head passed between them. The two men on the other side pulled their wires taut, and the Rex's head snapped in their direction. The scene played out as before, with the other two men diving away from the monster's powerful jaws. This repetitive circus wasn't getting them anywhere.

Before the others could take notice, Dot climbed over the railing and began lowering herself into the pit.

"Dot! What the hell are you doing?" Vic said when he noticed her dangling from the top of the wall.

Crow shook his head. "She crazier than I thought."

Vic scrambled off the railing, around his sister, and grabbed Dot's wrists. "If you go down there, that thing will eat you."

"No it won't. I can help."

"How the hell are you––"

"Vic," his sister said. "Let her go." Victoria had locked eyes with Dot.

"The hell you say." Vic scowled at Victoria, his eyelids pinched tight.

Seizing the opportunity, Dot released her hold on the wall and dropped. The sudden shift in weight––not to mention his lack of attention––caused Vic to lose his grip on her. Dot plummeted, her hands scraping against the cement wall as she fell. She hit the ground with a *thud*. A surge of pain rocketed up from her left ankle. Her vision went white. She dropped to her hands and knees.

"Fuck!"

She hadn't heard a snap, but her leg felt broken. She was afraid to look, not ready to see a snapped bone protruding from her skin. After a moment, she worked up the courage and check. Her ankle was swelling, but there weren't any bones visible. She figured she'd suffered no worse than a sprain.

Oh, thank God.

"Dot, move!" Victoria's harried warning came from the top of the wall. She was pointing at the Rex, who had taken notice of Dot's entrance and was lumbering towards her, dragging the mech with it. The power armor had released its hold on the creature's leg and had both arms clamped down on its tail. The armor's feet cut gouges in the earth as the beast dragged it along. The four men who had previously been holding the cables around the beast's neck were back upright, waving their arms and shouting for her to run.

Dot didn't run.

Here goes nothing.

Pushing to her feet and transferring the lion's share of her weight to her right leg, she hobbled toward the behemoth.

This is a terrible idea. The hell are you thinking?

The ground shook as the creature closed in on her, the tremors so fierce Dot nearly lost her balance. It didn't slow as it approached. It would use its velocity to scoop her into its maw and swallow her whole.

And just like that, this nightmare would be over.

Dot drew a long breath, held it, glared at the Rex, and said, "Stop!"

The Rex stopped.

It stood before her, panting, the energy it had spent fighting its captors fleeing all at once. Then, without another word from Dot, the king of the dinosaurs lowered its head––a mere foot away from Dot's scale-slippered feet––closed its eyes, and laid down before her.

Silence filled the habitat and the wall above. The onlookers watched with bulging eyes and hanging jaws, their minds unable to process what they'd just seen. There were no words. Just confusion and a quiet reverence.

"Well, fuck me sweetly with a steak knife," Crow said. "That crazy bitch weren't lyin.'"

CHAPTER 5

"I'll find a way." –Life

The great beast's flanks inflated and deflated as it calmly breathed. There were no white plumes of breath, though, because it was nowhere near cold enough. Somehow this disappointed Dot. She imagined a creature this big would have steaming breath even in the most tropical climes.

"Now I've seen it all," came a voice from behind Dot.

She dared to look away from the now docile Rex to see who had spoken.

For an instant, there was no one behind her; then a man of considerable build dropped into view. She glanced up at the wall he'd jumped down from, then back to him. He approached with his arm out, fist offered for a bump. She tentatively placed her fist against his before allowing her arm to flop back to her side.

"Leo Pride, at your service." The man was large, beastly even, with a flowing mane of blond hair. His skin was tanned nearly auburn, while his eyebrows were startlingly white. He wore brown and green combat fatigues, and weather-worn Doc Martens. Leo took a moment to pull his hair into a ponytail, removed a rubber band from his pocket, and tied his hair back. He did this with practiced motions, obviously used to fixing his 'do without the aid of a reflective surface. Yet Dot still cringed, imagining all the hairs that would be torn out when the guy finally removed the rubber band. Why didn't dudes think about such things?

"I'm Dot?" she said. Why it came out as a question was anyone's guess.

"Nice to meet you. Nifty talent you have there." He hitched his chin at the Rex. "How'd you come about it?"

"Newly discovered talent. And I haven't got a clue."

He shrugged. "Talent is talent. Welcome to Homosapien Park. I kinda run things around here."

Victor and Victoria both laughed from their place on the wall. Victor, in his joviality, almost fell off the wall, but Victoria grabbed him by the shoulder at the last minute and pulled him back. She said something Dot couldn't hear, but figured it was something like "Be careful" or "Dumbass."

"And what's so funny?" Leo said. His eyes were locked on Dot's, but he was obviously talking to the siblings.

"*Kinda run things?* Whatever. He's being modest," Victor called down.

"Where the fuck you been hiding, you coward?" Crow said before wrapping his arms around the man. How the soldier had gotten down here so fast, what with his shambling gait, Dot had no idea. He just sort of...*appeared*. She was reminded of those old slasher movies where the killer seemed to be everywhere the victim was, all at once, and had to push down some unease before it morphed into full-on fear.

"Just got back from the West. Scouting mission."

"Sah-weet." Crow, still hugging Leo, slapped at the bigger man's back. "Good to see you. How'd your scaredy-cat routine go?"

"Scoped nine 'dactyls doing circles off in the distance. Vulture bastards, the lot of them. No sign of the witch and her beast though."

Crow released the man and stepped back. "Must be nice living life through a telescopic lens while the rest of us fight these things face to face."

Crow and Leo laughed but Dot could sense the tension between the two. They seemed like friends, but you could never tell with men. They were, after all, the species that enjoyed kicking each other in the balls for shits and giggles.

"Wait," Dot said. "Didn't you shoot at Tutu from a tree-stand?"

"Was I talking to you?" Crow said.

Dot rolled her eyes.

"Anyway, scouting from afar is better than jerking off in the trenches," said Leo.

"Coward."

"Asshole."

Both men laughed again.

The Rex roared, and everyone in attendance jumped––aside from Foil, who remained safe and sound in his power armor.

"Hush!" Dot yelled over her shoulder.

The Rex's roar faded into an angry growl. Was the damn thing moping? It sure as hell looked that way. Its bottom lip—if that flap of scaly skin could be called a lip—poked out a bit. The big monster was acting like a toddler deprived of an afternoon snack.

"Nice shoes," Leo said. "Those from the East bitch?"

Dot nodded.

"Think that's why it's listening?" Leo asked.

"Don't know, don't care. As long as it's not eating us, I'm perfectly peachy."

"It made a helluva mess before you stopped it."

Dot couldn't tell if this Leo character was alluding to the idea that she could've acted sooner, or simply noting the gore-and-viscera-covered ground all around them. She'd never seen so much blood, guts, and ass strewn about, not even in war movies. The guy who'd been ripped into thirds: his jaw was working as if he were trying to say something, but his eyes were deader than King Tut. But the most staggering thing was that no one seemed all that upset over the loss of their comrades. How much death and carnage did someone have to witness before they reacted to a vicious mauling and trisection with apathy? Their indifference shook Dot to her core.

"I wasn't sure it would work," Dot said after a moment's reflection. She felt that honesty would win this guy over, and she was right.

"Fair enough." He nodded thoughtfully. "Says a lot about you."

"How so?"

"You jumped into a fight with a monster ten times your size, give or take, without being sure it wouldn't tear you apart."

"I've had...experiences with these things."

"Your little birddog?" Leo nodded at the raptor beside Dot.

"How'd you get down here?" Dot reached down and scratched the dino-doggo's head. "His name is Tutu," she said to Leo. "He's a good boy."

"YAP!"

"So he seems. Listen, I need to debrief my people. You down to hang around while that happens?"

"I don't have shit else to do besides figuring a way out of this hallucination."

Leo let out a mighty laugh. "I wish I were a figment of your imagination, Dot. I truly do. But this is all real. Question is, why don't you know that?"

"She landed here in a dumpster!" Victor called from the wall.

"Crushed the Eastern Witch flat!" Victoria yelled.

"That so?" Leo said.

Dot nodded.

"Fair play. A dumpster, you say?"

"I didn't say." She pointed to Victor. "He did."

"But a dumpster all the same?"

"Yes."

"Curiouser and curiouser."

"I never much cared for *Alice in Wonderland*."

"Shame. My kids loved it. Before they were eaten by a herd of allosauruses."

Dot flinched. "I'm...I'm so sorry."

"Got my wife, too. Cheapest divorce I've ever had." He said this with a straight face, but over his shoulder, Crow was stifling laughter with a gnarled fist.

Dot said, "I don't find that funny."

"Then you're gonna have a rough time here. Gallows humor is all we got, aside from each other, and most of these shitheads ain't even got shit for brains."

"Ain't that the truth!" Crow said as he burst into laughter.

Dot's face scrunched, like she smelled boiled dog shit. "You're both horrible."

Leo seemed to consider this. "Yes, yes we are. But you'd be horrible too if you'd spent the last year watching the people you love and care for become the bottom rung on the food chain. We laugh and joke to *maintain* our sanity, not because we've *lost it*. You'll see. You either toughen up, or you die."

"I'm tough enough, thanks."

Leo smiled. "I see that. Feel free to join us. Some bad shit is on the horizon, and we could use all the help we can get." What he said next was directed at Foil. "Get this big motherfucker secured."

"Uh..." Foil frowned. "How do you want me to do that, exactly?"

"It listens to Dot. You two figure it out. Retcon in twenty. Be there."

"Yessir."

With that, Leo turned and into a door set into the back of the exhibit's wall. Dot wondered if that was how Crow and Tutu had gotten down here so quickly without her noticing. All evidence seemed to point to such, at any rate.

"Excuse me, ma'am?" Foil said.

"Yeah, yeah, I heard him." Dot faced the Rex. She sighed and said, "Lay down."

The Rex fell over as if shoved. The ground trembled with the impact.

Dot went to the creature. She stood by its massive head, a cranium the size of a Mini Cooper, and whispered, "Go to sleep."

The Rex closed its eyes.

"Good girl."

"That's the freakiest shit I've ever seen. You think it's the shoes, like Leo said?" Foil asked.

"Who knows?"

"We'll secure him, either way. We got some guy wire that's as thick as my dick."

Her gaze shifted from his crotch back to the power armor. No doubt the guy was compensating for something. "That's a wonderful image, thanks. Be seeing you." Dot glanced down to where Tutu waited patiently by her side. "Come on, boy. Let's blow this joint."

"Hey!" Foil yelled as she turned away. "What if this thing wakes up before we get him tied down?"

"*He* is a *her*, and if she wakes up you can beat her unconscious with that dick of yours."

§ § §

Crow wouldn't allow Tutu inside where the humans were, no matter how much Dot tried to convince him that the dino-dog was harmless as long as she had the shoes on.

"Don't care. He could be dead as a fuckin' doornail and I still wouldn't let you bring him in. When it's a choice between safe and sorry, I always vote safe. The mutt stays out here. With me."

Tutu whined, as if he'd understood the entire back and forth. He rubbed his head against Dot's leg, and Dot leaned down to pet him.

"Stay out here and keep an eye on that big son of a bitch over there, alright? That's a good boy."

Victor and Victoria led Dot in the direction Leo had disappeared, through the door at the rear of the exhibit. Victor held the door open while Victoria and Dot moseyed inside.

The corridor they entered was long and devoid of life, with plain cinder-block walls, and bulbs dangling from extension cords anchored to the ceiling at ten-foot intervals––five lights in all. The floors were smooth concrete, the kind you'd find in a distribution center, like Sam's Club, or even your local Walmart, and the trio's shoes made hollow slaps as they walked. Two doors sat on the right, none on the left, with a single door at the end of the hallway, all three painted different colors. The first on the right was blue, the second red, the one at the end orange.

Dot followed the siblings to the orange door, where Victor once again played gentleman, holding the door open for the ladies.

Inside, banquet tables were arranged in a four-by-four grid pattern with four chairs facing the same direction on one side, and no chairs at all on the other; all eyes were on the podium at the back wall. Leo stood behind the makeshift pulpit, studying something on the stand in front of him. He didn't so much as look up to acknowledge their presence.

He waved a hand in their general direction. "Have a seat. We'll be starting in fifteen."

Dot and the siblings took seats at the front left table, leaving one chair open at the end for whoever wanted it. Over the course of the next ten minutes, people shuffled in, every one of them looking haggard, unkempt to the point that Dot could imagine what they smelled like before their body odor hit her. When the smell did strike, the reality was much worse than her imaginings. Animalistic, was the best way to describe the aroma wafting from their filthy bodies. Aptly enough, they smelled like an ape exhibit at the zoo. For a brief second, Dot toyed with the thought that, if dogs had been changed into dinosaurs, what had apes been turned into? Humans maybe? Had all of these people been apes before the change? She doubted it. For one, they all spoke English, or so she had to assume, because they understood Leo just fine. For two, she still didn't buy the idea that some magic spell cast by a pair of witches had changed the world like it had. There was no such thing as magic. Then Dot remembered the odd placement of the stars she'd seen earlier and considered the possibility that, in this world, maybe magic *could* be real.

"Do you guys not have running water?" Dot whispered. The smell was getting to her.

"Nope," said Victor.

Victoria said, "We take a group bath in the otter exhibit every time it rains, which is about once a week this time of year, but other than that, we don't have access to fresh water. And we ran out of soap nine months ago. Same with deodorant and the like."

"What the hell do you drink?" asked Dot.

"Foil set up condensation rigs on the roofs." Victoria pointed to the ceiling, as if Dot could see through walls. "They also collect rainwater. But we don't use that for hygiene purposes, for obvious reasons."

"Don't wanna run out," Victor added.

Dot grimaced. "Yuck."

"Yuck?" Victoria said. "You say that like we have a choice. This is the best-case scenario, given the state of the world. Besides, a little dirt never hurt anyone. I've gotten used to the smell, and you will too."

"Unlikely." Dot took a deep breath through her mouth and instantly regretted it. The room had the kind of stench you could taste. She half expected to see a noxious cloud of green funk clinging silent but deadly to the bodies of everyone in view, like they were a bunch of toxic Pigpens. Dot wondered why she hadn't smelled the siblings, or Crow for that matter, while she was outside, and figured it had something to do with open-air versus confined spaces.

Crow, Foil, and one other man Dot hadn't been introduced to yet arrived next. Crow took the seat at the end of their table, while Foil and the unnamed man sat with other strangers at the next table over. Once they were settled, Leo began.

"I have bad news, and I have worse news. Folks like Crow might think it's good news, but I don't share his enthusiasm. We have gathering forces in the West, and I can only assume it's due to our newest arrival—" Leo made quick eye contact with Dot before looking out over the small group of people once more "—having murdered the West's sister."

"No way news travelled that fast, right?" Victor asked.

"We're dealing with witches, Vic," said Victoria. "They gotta have some kind of connection us normies don't."

"Ah, yeah, I guess you're right. Go on, Leo. Sorry to interrupt."

"You're fine, Vic. It was a good question." Leo cleared his throat. "We have 'dactyls circling the Ape Grounds. And the apes are—"

"Apes?" Dot asked.

"When the world changed, dogs became dinosaurs, and cats became primordial apes, you know, like they do." Victor flashed a goofy smile.

"Cats became apes? What kinda sense..."

"May I continue?" Leo asked from the podium.

"Yeah, yeah, whatever." Dot sat back in her chair, shaking her head to clear it. The nonsensical state of the world was completely mind-boggling.

Leo went on. "The Ape Grounds have been growing increasingly unstable as the bitch in the West encroaches on their territory. The Apes don't like us, and neither does she, but the enemy of our enemy is not our friend."

Crow said, "You ain't sayin' shit we don't already know."

"Hush, man," Victoria said, "Dot doesn't know this."

Dot rolled her eyes. "I feel like a character in a portal fantasy."

"Ain't far from the truth, is it?" Victor said with a grin.

"I stand corrected. Please, for the love of fuck, continue," Dot told Leo.

"Thank you. As I was saying, the Apes are becoming more aggravated, and the arrival of the 'dactyls overhead isn't helping. It can only be assumed that the West is planning to overtake the Ape Grounds. Question is, do we let that happen? Or do we help them?"

"Help them?!" cried a woman Dot didn't have a name for. The lady's face was smeared with what seemed to be soot. She looked like she belonged in a depression-era photograph. "They killed a dozen of us the first month we were here, Leo!"

"Don't you think I know that? One of those was a good friend of mine, a brother. But, if we help them, they might help us in return."

"You're talking about mindless monkeys, champ," said Foil. "They'd rip the opposable thumbs right off us and shove 'em up our asses as quick as look at us. I ain't risking what few lives we got left on a hunch, no matter how much I respect you."

Dot glanced around the room, counting heads. Aside from the occupied chairs, there were six people standing against the far wall, each one dirtier than the next. This couldn't be all of the survivors, right? The population of Homosapien Park surely couldn't be the only numbers humanity had left. Instead of assuming, Dot raised her hand.

Leo acknowledged her. "Yes?"

"Is this it? Is this all of you?"

Leo looked around, seemed to count everyone in attendance. "We're short one but yeah."

Foil said, "We ain't short one, Leo. Larry got ate."

"Shit. Yeah. Sorry." Leo frowned. "Then, yes, this is all of us."

"What about the rest of the world?" Dot asked.

"I wouldn't know. We've not had contact with anyone for six months. Last communication we had was with a base in China's Wuhan Province. But they've been silent for half a year."

Dot leaned forward. "There's gotta be more humans left than this."

Leo shook his head slowly. "I really don't think there is."

"Jesus Christ, are you for real?"

"Yeah," Victoria said, "he is."

"There's only," she did the quick math in her head, "*twenty of you?*"

"Twenty-one, now," Victor said, smiling. "You know, counting you."

"For fuck's sake..." Dot considered all the information she'd received until this point and said, "How many apes?"

"Couple hundred," Crow said.

"More than that." Leo placed his palms flat on the podium. "They've been growing in numbers recently. This past spring was one big orgy out there. Every female in the group was pregnant. All those younguns are old enough to fight now. They're still children, but they're a threat nonetheless."

"You wanna take twenty people to war with hundreds of apes?" Dot asked, perplexed by the insanity of Leo's plan.

"No. I don't want to fight them, if possible. If we help defend their land, they might help us." Leo said.

Dot laughed. "I agree with these other folks. You're crazy."

"Do you have a better idea?"

Dot considered something that had been brewing in the back of her mind ever since Leo had first mentioned his plan.

"Yeah," she said, "I think I do."

CHAPTER 6

Hi-Yo, Silver!

You can't possibly be serious." Victoria followed Dot into the little girls' room. She rested her hands against a sink behind her and glared at Dot as she entered a stall. "That's your plan?"

"Yup." Dot cringed as she hovered over the disgusting toilet. She disliked peeing with other people in the room, especially when she knew they were listening.

"You're just going to walk over there with a couple dinosaurs in tow, cross your fingers, hold your breath, and hope your little shoes can convince a couple hundred killer apes not to rip you apart?"

"Again, yup," Dot said, while instinctively flushing the toilet. When nothing happened, she sighed. She exited the stall and approached the sink next to Victoria. Again, she absentmindedly turned on the faucet, expecting a rush of water. Nothing.

Jesus Christ, how have these heathens survived without running water?

"That's insane. Do you know how insane that sounds?" Victoria shook her head. "What if it doesn't work?"

"I'll have Tutu and Sue to back me up."

Victoria knitted her brows into a scowl. "Who the fuck is Sue?"

Dot frowned at the girl. "My new dino friend. Sue the T-Rex. Get it?"

"No, I don't *get it*. That's a stupid name for a tyrannosaurus."

Shrugging, Dot started for the exit. "Take it up with the people at the Field Museum."

"What?" Victoria said, following. "Look, I don't care about the damn thing's name. What I care about is you being killed by a bunch of knuckle-dragging monsters."

"Do you have a better idea?" Dot was heading back to the mess hall. She'd needed some supplies before setting out on what was most assuredly a suicide mission.

Victoria caught up and inserted herself between Dot and the door. "Yeah," she said, "Leo's plan. We all go."

Hands on her hips, one eyebrow arched, Dot said, "That's just stupid. If the worst happens, humanity will be wiped out. How would that help anyone?"

Victoria fumbled for an answer.

"Exactly. Now, can you get out of my way?" When Victoria didn't budge, Dot reached around her for the handle and pushed past. The mess hall was empty. Dot stepped in, scanned the room, and glanced back at Victoria. "Where'd everybody go?"

Leaning against the doorway, Victoria said, "To bed. Lights out at nine."

"The fuck? What kind of childish shit is that?"

"Foil cuts the power to conserve energy." She nodded toward the hallway. "Look, you don't have to go to sleep, but you're gonna be in the dark, so you might as well get some rest, right?"

Dot huffed. She hadn't gone to bed by nine since she was a child, well before she came to live with her aunt and uncle. But though she wouldn't admit it out loud, a good night's sleep did sound pretty damn good.

Maybe I'll wake up back in my bed, and this nightmare will be over.

Victoria took Dot's hand and led them toward the barracks. Dot rolled her eyes but allowed herself to be pulled down the corridor. Besides, she kind of liked holding Victoria's hand. Out of everyone here, Dot had grown closest to Victoria, for whatever reason. Probably because she was the only other woman Dot had spoken to. But Dot thought it might be something more than that. Like the fact that Victoria was cute––or at least she would be, after a long, hot shower.

Eventually, they arrived at a pair of doors on opposite walls. Someone had spray painted *Dudes* on one and *Chicas* on the other.

Classy. At that point, though, it was what Dot had come to expect. After all, these were the same idiots who named the last bastion of humanity *Homo Park*. What a bunch of fucking hillbillies. She wasn't dealing with Rhodes scholars, that was for sure.

Bunkbeds lined the walls of the dormitory, all of them crude structures made of black and copper pipe and PVC, held together with duct tape, shoelaces, and aspirations. They'd obviously been built by the remaining survivors.

Only a handful of the beds were occupied. The male survivors outnumbered the woman four-to-one. If she didn't know better, Dot would have said it was an apocalypse engineered by a bunch of misogynists. She didn't want to consider how this sausage-fest was going to go about rebuilding society. The pressure the remaining women felt to continue the species must have been crippling. Dot wondered if she'd be willing to bed a man simply to procreate, and shook her head at the prospect. She was more than a baby factory. If she chose a man, cool. If not, the first guy to force himself on her would go away missing numerous parts of his anatomy.

Releasing Dot's hand, Victoria skipped across the room towards a pair of unoccupied beds. "Top or bottom?" she said. "I usually take top, but you're our guest, so you can pick."

"I'm not usually a bottom girl." Dot smirked, then eyed the *bed* to Victoria's right. "I'll take that one."

"Guess we can both be on top then."

Dot grimaced, but the look was lost to the sudden onset of darkness.

She wasn't kidding about cutting the power.

No one in the room had turned off the lights. The power had been shut off from the outside.

After a moment, Dot's eyes adjusted.

Faint moonlight poured in from small rectangular windows near the ceiling, all of them barren of coverings. Dot couldn't imagine being locked in here beyond bedtime. The place was a volunteer prison––though, maybe saying these people *volunteered* to sleep here was pushing it. Where else would they sleep? Oddly enough, what bothered her the most were the missing curtains. The sun in the morning was going to be a problem, even for an early riser like Dot. Farm life, can you dig it?

Looks like we'll be up at first light. Just like back home.

She sighed as she sat on the bottom bunk and slipped off her shoes. She was about to slide them under the bed, then stopped herself. She reached down. Her two new friends—Tutu and Sue—might have been locked up, but what if something happened? What if they got loose? Or worse, what if the compound was attacked by a herd of angry dinos?

What's a herd of dinosaurs actually called? Does it change based on the species? Do they even flock together? Flock. Is that what you'd call a group of pterodactyls?

Furthermore, if she kept her shoes off, would the spell break? Would Sue come back to herself and eat Tutu whole?

Shit, I can't let that *happen—*

"Good night," Victoria said, interrupting Dot's ramblings.

Dot retrieved the shoes and slid them back on. "Night," she said and climbed to the top bunk. She'd never slept with shoes on before, not while sober anyway. Then again, she'd never needed to. She didn't bother pulling back the covers; she rolled on to her side and promptly fell asleep.

§ § §

Sunlight poured in through the windows, so bright Dot could see it through her eyelids. She bolted upright, hoping to see the faded One Direction poster across from her bed, the pictures of friends tucked between her dresser's mirror and frame, the cheap plywood desk and her Black Friday Walmart laptop. But as the haze of sleep receded, the women's dorm sprawled out before her, every bed vacant. She eyed Victoria's bunk. The sheets were pulled up and tucked under the pillow. The other bunks were in varying states of disarray.

Where the hell is everyone? What time is it?

The hallway was as empty as the room she'd left behind; the men's dorm too, and both bathrooms. *What the fuck?* She glanced at her scaly green shoes. *Did that bitch cast another spell, turning all the humans into ants, or something?* Approaching the mess hall, she held her breath and threw the door open.

Half-a-dozen heads turned to face her. Apparently, Dot had slept through breakfast and almost past lunch. Most of the late eaters were parked at a single table. One, however, stood at the back of the room, in front of a table that sat perpendicular to the others. Dot recognized the man, or at least thought she did, but she wasn't sure why. In his late forties, bald, he had the beginnings of a gut hanging over his belt.

"Hey, Dot," the man said. "Hungry?" He hefted a cheese sandwich from a haphazard pile in the center of the table and held it out to her. Not a grilled cheese, mind you. A plain, white bread and American cheese sandwich.

As soon as he spoke, she recognized his voice. "Foil?"

Screwing up his face and landing on a frown, he said, "Last I checked."

"Sorry." Dot accepted the sandwich and grabbed a warm, off-brand lemon-lime soda can from an aluminum pyramid situated next to the mound of toddler food. "I couldn't see your face yesterday, you know, through your… power armor? What is that thing, anyway?"

"Newt." He motioned toward a nearby table. "I call her Newt."

The fuck kind of name is Newt? Wait. Wasn't that the name of—

"I built the original version in my garage," Foil said. "Would've been the raddest cosplay at Comicon last year. Then, this happened." He looked around the room, his eyes cold, filled with disdain. "I stripped off the nonessential parts, added the armor plating, and the rest, as they say, is the fuckin' dino-dog apocalypse."

"I see." Dot bit off a corner of her sandwich. It was the blandest thing she'd ever put in her mouth, while at the same time being delicious. She couldn't shovel it in fast enough. *How long has it been since I last ate?*

"So, you're into comics?" she said, her mouth full, crumbs falling from her lips.

Foil popped open her soda can, followed by his own. "Used to be," he said. "Had a shitload back in mom's…" He paused, considered Dot for a moment. "But that's ancient history."

His face fell, and she could almost see the memories cycling through his gray matter. She'd always found grown men who were sad far more depressing than sorrowful women. What that said about her, she didn't have the foggiest. Maybe she felt like women's natural state of being was depressed? What with the patriarchy and all that? Constantly being stepped on because of her gender sucked, so why shouldn't men be happier? Dot thought she'd be fucking chipper as hell, too, if she ruled the goddamn world.

"Well, it looks like your hobby turned out to be pretty useful." She grabbed her can and took a long drink. The warm fizz coated her throat and stomach and set her skin tingling. It was like drinking a soda for the first time. If she closed her eyes, she could almost pretend it was cold enough to be refreshing.

"I guess." He took a swig from his can, sloshed the bubbles around, and swallowed hard. "If I'd have been home when the bitches cast their spell, I might have been able to save mom from Pooky."

Dot coughed, covered her mouth. "Pooky?"

"Her labradoodle. She loved that damn dog, right up until he ate her."

Dot nodded and looked away, stifling a laugh. Foil's tale was horrible, sure, but Dot couldn't help but imagine a labradoodle with scales instead of fur ripping someone apart. It was like imagining a sword fight between a bobby pin and a claymore, and the bobby pin winning. She shoved the rest of her sandwich into her mouth and chewed. Slow and methodical. Focusing on mastication aided in repressing her need to laugh out loud.

"Where is everyone?" she said before taking another drink.

Foil chugged the rest of his soda, then crushed the can in his hand. "Prepping for the hunt."

"What hunt?"

"For Donkey Kong." He tossed the mangled can over his shoulder.

"What?" Dot shot to her feet. Her folding chair crashed to the floor, startling the others. "That plan was crap. I told Leo I'd handle it on my own."

Foil bit into the middle of the sandwich and chewed like a man trying to make a point--though, Dot had no idea what that point was.

"That's true," he said, shifting the food to one cheek and talking out the other side. "But we all thought your plan was crap, too. So we vetoed it."

"Fuck's sake. Where are they?"

"Probably in the T-Rex pit making their final preparations."

"The pit? Why there? What are they doing to Sue?"

"Sue?" Foil arched an eyebrow then shook his head. "Never mind, I don't want to know."

"Foil. What. Are. They. *Doing*?"

He grinned, a piece of cheese plastering a front tooth. "It's a surprise, Dot."

Dot huffed, turned, and stormed out of the mess.

§ § §

Surprise, my ass.

Dot marched down the hall, her footfalls heavy, each stomp reverberating up the walls. They were going to kill Sue. *What else could he have meant?* They'd shoot her, lop her head off, and mount it on a plaque like some sick trophy––the Wicked Rex of the East in all her glory. *Look how manly I look standing next to a dead living thing. Surely this has lengthened the size of my penis three sizes this day!*

Wait. Why do I care? She's just some stupid dino.

A dino that ate someone while Dot watched, no less.

Sue had it coming.

But somehow Dot felt responsible for her. Almost protective.

The fuck's that about?

She was a few feet from the door leading to the pit when Sue unleashed a thunderous roar from the other side. Dot stopped cold. Her teeth clattered, hairs standing up on her forearms.

Oh, God. They're torturing her.

No creature deserved that. Well, maybe those three assholes who chased her into that alley and sent her on this wild ride. Those shitheels had died way too quickly for Dot's liking.

The corridor shook as Sue slammed her foot into the ground. The door rattled in its frame. Dust sprang free from the overhead lights. The image of Leo lying under Sue's foot filled Dot's head; his eyes and mouth exploding with blood as the nine-ton lizard crushed his chest. She smirked. The king of the jungle vs the queen of the dinosaurs.

No chance, Simba.

Another roar. This one twinged with pain.

Dot kicked the door open and yelled, "What the hell's going on?"

Every head in the pit snapped in her direction, Sue's included. Then, the great beast gave a little whine and bent her head like a dog afraid of its master's ire.

Two men Dot didn't know stood on either side of the dinosaur, each one brandishing a handmade spear. Crow was about ten yards to Dot's left, his rifle leveled at Sue's head. Victor and Leo were on Sue's back, attaching something to her midsection. The wires around the creature's neck, the ones Foil had fastened to the D-rings cemented into the ground, were the only things keeping the five fucktards alive.

Is that a saddle?

"Is that a fuckin' saddle?" Dot did a double take. It *was* a saddle. The two knuckleheads on Sue's back had just finished buckling it when Dot barged out into the crowd.

"Oh hey, Dot," Vic said. He smiled and gave a little wave. "And yeah, it's a saddle. You like it?"

"Like it? You put...a saddle...on a T-Rex. A *saddle*."

Vic's smile faded. He climbed down and wandered in Dot's direction, dragging his feet. "You don't like it?"

"You put a saddle on the most terrifying creature known to man, what's not to like?" Dot couldn't bring herself to make eye contact with the young man making puppy dog eyes at her. Her gaze was fixed on Sue and the leather contraption fixed to her back.

"Oh." Victor stopped, his brow furled, lips pulled tight. "I thought—"

"That I was pissed?" She finally met his gaze.

"Yeah."

Dot frowned and shook her head. "Nah, I'm not mad. I'm fucking dumbfounded. You guys are fucking morons. Which one of you idiots thought you could ride this thing? She'd pluck you off her back as soon as she was free and devour you like Steve."

"Larry," Leo said, hopping off Sue's back. "She ate Larry."

"Like it fuckin' matters."

Victor stepped between Dot and Leo, waving his hands. "We weren't going to try to ride her. The saddle's for you."

"For..." Dot squinted at Victor then shifted her gaze to Leo. "I thought you didn't like my plan? Foil said you all vetoed it."

"We did." Leo stepped up next to Victor, arms crossed over his chest. "But I figured you'd just go behind our backs and do it anyway. At least this way, you can do so with style." He gave her a stupid grin, and it took every ounce of willpower to keep from slapping it off his stupid face. "Plus," he continued, "if things do go sideways, you'll have a much better chance of escaping. On foot, those apes would be on you faster than a democrat on socialism."

Dot let the asinine remark go and glanced at Victor, who was smiling at her again, then back to Leo. "When do I leave?"

"Soon as you're ready." Said Leo. "Victoria's putting some provisions together for you. The apes are about a day's ride, so you'll need enough food to get there and back."

"What's the catch?" Dot planted her hands on her hips. "You're being *way* too accommodating."

"No catch. As much as I don't like it, you and your fancy shoes are probably our only chance of surviving. So it's a risk I'm willing to take. I just hope you're right about them working on those hairy motherfuckers."

He was lying. Dot knew it, and she knew he knew she knew it.

CHAPTER 7

Girl Scout

Victoria arrived shortly after Dot had been given the news that she would be leading the charge (or breaking away from the group, if she was honest with herself) and handed over the backpack full of provisions Leo had mentioned. It was a child's backpack: plastic, shiny, some cartoon character's mug sown into the flap so that the vinyl patch bulged along with the toon's eyes. Some kind of square yellow creature with blue shorts; or perhaps, since he was so short, capris or pants. She was sure she knew the character's name, but it just wasn't coming to her.

"Cute," Dot said as she slung the pack over one shoulder. There was no way she'd be able to fit her other arm through the provided strap, the pack was so small. Still, it felt loaded to bursting with supplies.

"It's the best we have. Everyone else will be using their own duffels and purses and whatnot in case we need to leave to give you backup." Victoria frowned at the last word: *backup*. She looked frightened and more than a little like she was holding something back.

"You got something you wanna to tell me?" Dot asked. She wasn't normally so gentle with her prying, being of the mind that upfront honesty was the best policy and should be uttered with haste, but there was something… *fragile* about the young woman before her. Dot felt that if she pressed even a little, Victoria would run off, tears streaming and mouth screaming. It was the last thing she wanted, and that was likely when it all began. A signal sparking in the back of Dot's mind. Was there a chance…?

"I don't have any friends here," Victoria said. Her voice was soft, sincere, guarded. "I got Victor, and he's my best friend, but he's family first. I don't much care for anyone else, not in a friendly way, anyhow. Well, not in any kind of way, really. I was kinda hoping…that we could be friends? I like how forthright you are, how you don't take anyone's crap." Victoria glanced at the saddled and docile Rex behind Dot. "But if you go and get yourself killed, who knows when, or even *if*, someone else will show up. Even if they do, it'll likely be a guy. I just…I want a gal pal, you know?"

Dot considered this. "I like you, Victoria. *When* I make it back—" she stressed the *when* by leaning in, coming nearly nose-to-nose with the other woman, close enough to kiss "—we'll talk about this some more. Okay?" Dot felt an uncharacteristic need to pat Victoria on the arm, or even give the woman a hug, but she respected Victoria's space. If she wanted human contact, Victoria would have to instigate it.

"Okay," Victoria said with a small smile, but her eyes doubted every word Dot had said. Even with their melancholy cast, Victoria's eyes twinkled, and Dot found herself unwilling to break contact with them. The spell was finally broken by the raucous growl of machinery.

Foil had hopped inside Newt and started it up. The power armor whirred to life, servos and hydraulics whining and pumping. He lay one of the massive pincer arms on the ground, like a cashier will hold out a hand awaiting payment, and Dot climbed aboard. Newt ground and squeaked as it lifted her aloft. The ride was shaky, to say the least, but Dot had found a caution-stripped handhold to grasp, on which she could steady herself. Foil got her as close to the calm T-Rex as he could without touching its flank; Dot watched in wonder, and with a modicum of fear, as the Rex's side inflated and deflated with breath. She positioned herself where she could keep hold of the handrail on the mech's arm while she slipped one foot into the left stirrup, then released the bar so she could swing into the seat on the Rex's back. With ease, she placed her right foot into its corresponding stirrup, sat back, and assessed her mount.

She couldn't see shit. The saddle rested on the dino's back, just above the hips, giving Dot an up-close-and-personal view of the creature's minute shoulder blades and scaly flesh. She leaned to and fro, trying to look around the monster, but it was too wide. Perhaps this was a stupid idea after all. At the very least, it hadn't been well thought out.

"Bit like riding a horse blindfolded, I'd assume," Leo called from the ground.

"This ain't gonna work," Dot said.

"It'll have to. If you want to go ahead with your plan, that is."

Dot thought that this had maybe been Leo's plan all along. Get the little lady up on her new pet dino and show her how silly she was being, thinking she could scout out a location, much less be the vanguard of this patchwork army he'd assembled. She despised him in that moment: his smug expression (real or imagined), the knowing grin at the corner of his mouth. He was every man she'd ever met, explaining something obvious to her in great detail: Uncle Heinrich making sure she understood the difference between the brake and the gas pedal; the man they bought feed from informing her that the chicken feed was for chickens, and the deer corn was for deer; her third grade teacher, Mr. Arnold, asking her what the largest organ on the human body was. "Your flesh," she'd answered. "Nope. It's your skin." She'd followed up with, "What's the difference?" and Mr. Arnold had responded, "Moving on. Mark, what is the—"

"I'm good. I'm gonna treat her like one of my uncle's mares, and hope she has some semblance of self-preservation when it comes to not running into trees, or off cliffs for that matter."

Leo didn't look disappointed. Only amused. "Then ride out. Oh, and there's a walkie in the supplies I asked Victoria to pack for you. Told her to leave it off. We'll leave ours on and plugged into the backup power supply. If you need us, give us a squawk. Cool?"

"Sounds like a plan."

"Good luck," Leo said, and looked like he meant it. There was no sarcasm or mockery in his tone, but something still felt...*off*. The feeling that she was being kept in the dark about something important niggled at her. It was an annoying sensation, but what was she going to do? Come right out and ask him what he was hiding? He'd lie through those perfect teeth of his, and she'd lose any chance of closing the gap between the two of them and, in doing so, cut off all chances of learning anything more than she already knew.

"See ya soon," she said, and clicked her tongue in the same way she used to with Uncle's Henrich's mare.

"Long days and pleasant nights!" Victor hollered. He waved goofily, his limp wrist flopping this way and that. The cheesy grin on his face caused Dot to sigh, the same way she did when she saw a certain president's name on signs in people's front yard.

Bless his heart...

The Rex lumbered forward. Dot maintained her hold on the saddle grip, but just barely. Riding on the massive beast was far more awkward than she could've ever imagined. One hip would come up, threatening to spill her off one side, only for it to dip low a split second before she fell, rocking her back in the other direction. Riding Sue wasn't anything like riding one of Uncle Heinrich's mares. It was more like trying to stay upright on the bridge of a ship during a hurricane.

"Hi-yo, Silver, away!" Victor shrieked.

"Nerd," was the last thing Dot heard as the Rex got going.

§ § §

Tutu followed Dot and Sue for a while before going off on his own. Dot wanted to call after her companion, tell him to heel, or some shit, but she figured the little guy must be hungry. She'd let him hunt, or whatever it was he needed to do, in peace.

Dot had never been good with distance travelled. She knew it was half a mile to the corner store from home, and another mile farther to the burger joint where she'd just been hired in her previous life——also known as yesterday. Or real life. Whichever fit here. So unsurprisingly, how long she'd been on the Rex's back was also a mystery. This was about the time when a watch or phone would have come in handy. The only passage of time she was privy to *here* was the sun moving over the trees and into the sky overhead, and that told her a great big ball of fuck-all.

Starting and stopping the Rex was as easy as clicking her tongue, but Dot thought it had much more to do with some kind of psychic bond between her and the creature she rode, something powered by the shoes she'd stolen off the dead witch that'd been crushed under Dumpster Flight 001. Dot hadn't eaten anything for breakfast, so she stopped once *Homo Park* was out of sight. She pulled her pack around, pinching it between her stomach and the Rex's back, and slid the zipper open. There was a cheese sandwich: homemade bread and cheese stacked together, cold and uninviting. The cheese wasn't square or round. It was blob shaped and kind of looked like Europe, if the boot that was Italy jutted from the top like some gimpy horn. The cheese must have been homemade by someone back at the park. What milk they'd used was anyone's guess, and Dot tried her damnedest not to consider the idea that it might be human breast milk. The only comfort she could give herself was that none of the women were pregnant. Though of course, you didn't have to be pregnant to lactate...

She tore off Italy and chewed the salty section of boot-shaped cheese.

It didn't taste any different from, say, a Kraft single, although if it *was* breast milk, would she really notice? She hadn't been breast fed as a child––not that she'd be able to remember that anyway––due to terrible reflux that was exacerbated by dairy, so she had no metric by which to discern breast milk from cow's milk, or any other animal's milk for that matter. It also meant she could look forward to a tummy ache in a couple hours. But what else was she going to eat?

After all that internal dialogue, Dot settled on thinking of the cheese, oddly shaped or not, as a good old-fashioned slice of the processed cheese product that America had seen fit to name after itself.

While she devoured her sandwich, she checked the remaining contents of the child's backpack. She found a flashlight, the walkie Leo had mentioned, and a buck knife in a rawhide sheath. All of it sat on top of what appeared to be a bedroll. A second cheese sandwich and a bottle of water that'd had its label peeled off ages ago were stuffed down one side of the pack. The water bottle was sticky where glue had once held the label in place, but it left no residue on Dot's hand after she drank from it. She stuffed the remainder of her cold cheese sandwich in her mouth and chased it with a slug of water, then returned the sticky bottle to the spot alongside the bedroll and zipped up the pack.

She clicked her tongue, spurring the Rex onward, her hand white-knuckle tight on the hard knob at the front of the saddle.

The sun was high, warming her shoulders where her shirt didn't cover the skin. As the duo progressed through fields and trees alike, Dot saw numerous smaller dinosaurs here and there, but nothing she'd consider a threat to her or Sue. The T-Rex was likewise unimpressed with the flora and fauna they came across. Regret churned in the back of her mind, though; a warm voice that reprimanded her for not paying more attention in school where dinosaurs were concerned. She'd thought, *I'm never going to use this information*, and that was that. It was the same reason she hadn't taken Calculus and Physics.

She stared at the great expanse of blue above her as she rode her great lizard steed. Not a cloud dotted the sky. No planes. No birds...

She clicked her tongue again and the Rex came to a shuddering halt. She remained focused on the sky above, the information she'd garnered up until now swirling in her head.

Where were the birds? Her new friends (companions?) had told her what had become of the dogs and cats of the world, but what about the birds? She'd seen dark shapes burst from the trees the night she'd arrived, but in this new weird and wacky world, they could've been anything. For that matter, what about every other animal? Giraffes, elephants, gophers? What about insects? Was it only humans that weren't affected? Cows? Chickens? Once again, she pondered where the group had gotten the milk to make cheese, or the eggs needed for bread. Dinosaurs laid eggs, but they didn't produce milk. Or did they? Her brain reeled as it searched for answers. If only she'd paid more attention in school.

Wait. Hadn't one of the twins mentioned that the dinos had attacked the animals in the zoo? That would mean they hadn't all——

A cry sounded from somewhere ahead. Dot snapped her gaze from sky to ground, hunting for the origin of the wail.

She was in a clearing, surrounded by trees on all sides. The field stretched out around her, and she guessed she could have easily fit Fenway Park within the provided acreage.

Off in the distance, maybe a hundred yards away, stood a hunched figure Dot placed instantly. She'd seen all the new *Planet of the Apes* movies and had watched enough Discovery Channel in her day to know an ape when she saw one. And that's all she saw, too: just the one.

Where are your friends, Bobo, my dear?

Leo had said it was a day's ride to the Ape Land, or whatever he'd called it. She knew she hadn't been riding all day, even if she had no way to tell time.

Then it hit her. Hard.

"You're out here for the same reason I am," she said aloud yet to herself. "You're a scout."

If the ape heard her at this distance, he or she was unbothered by her statement. It simply lurked and stared, probably assessing whether investigating a woman riding a massive killing machine was worth the risk. Then it spun with impressive speed and dashed into the trees, where it vanished. Even at this distance, Dot could hear the thing fleeing through the woods, snapping branches and skating through forest-floor detritus, until the sounds of its escape first dwindled then disappeared altogether.

"Go on. Go tell your buddies I'm coming. I—"

The Rex reared and roared. Dot threw herself forward, one hand on the saddle's leathery knob, the other wrapped as far around the Rex's neck as was possible, which wasn't much. The beast lurched forward, dashing in the direction which the ape had disappeared. Dot could only hold on and pray, and she wasn't much for prayer.

The Rex raced across the clearing and barreled into the tree line. Branches and leaves snatched at Dot's bare forearms, breaking the skin and sending rivulets of blood down her flesh. She bit her bottom lip to keep from crying out and spooking (or angering) the creature further. She lost what little grip she had on the Rex's neck and her arm shot into the air over her head. She was sure she looked like a rodeo clown because, in truth, she felt like one. Forcing her arm back down, she dug her fingers under the edge of the saddle and held on for dear life.

Primordial screeching echoed all around her. The woods were alive with the noise of feral primates. Even over the thundering footfalls of her mount, Dot could hear the excited and perhaps even fearful screams of what could only be apes––hundreds of them. How many had Leo said there were? Again, she chided herself for not paying more attention.

The Rex burst from the forest and came to a sliding halt. Dot peeled herself off the dinosaur's neck and sat back in the saddle, surveying her new surroundings.

A suburban street, no different from a thousand others like it, sat all around her. Tract houses, overgrown with grass and weeds and shrubs, lined either side of a cracked and detritus-littered road. No cars in sight. No people either. Not that she'd been expecting any. But that didn't mean the place wasn't occupied. It had its residents, even if they weren't human, and they were legion.

The apes came from the houses in single file lines. Each one was naked, something Dot noted only because she wouldn't have been surprised to see them all in jeans and graphic tees, or khakis and Hawaiian shirts. Nothing would've surprised her at this point in her adventures. Anything was possible in this funhouse-mirror of a world into which she'd been thrust, and finding the apes unclothed seemed genuinely out of place. She expected Beaver Cleaver-era apes, running around in propellor hats, and families of primates gathered around dinner tables with suckling pigs as center pieces.

Witches bless us, everyone...

She counted maybe a dozen apes per house, some no bigger than a human toddler, while others were the size of gorillas, if they weren't *actual* gorillas. She was, of course, no expert. She didn't know the difference between a baboon and an orangutan, much less the chasm between an ape and a gorilla. She *did* know that gorillas were huge, though, and some of these motherfuckers were the breadth of rhinos. She couldn't imagine what she'd do if one of them charged her——forgetting for a moment that she was on the back of one of the most dangerous predators of all time.

One of the apes——or maybe a chimpanzee? She only knew *that* species because of those old Clint Eastwood comedies her uncle loved watching—— moved in her direction, using its overlong forearms to swing itself across the sun-sparkled tarmac. The chimp stopped in the middle of the street and waved Dot over.

Waved.

Her.

Over.

Like a friend who'd been waiting for her to arrive for most of the day.

Like her aunt when dinner was ready.

The gesture was so strikingly human that Dot forgot again that she was ten feet in the air, sitting in a saddle on the back of a Tyrannosaurus Rex. She made to swing out of the saddle, as if it lay on nothing more than one of Henrich's mares, and stopped herself just short of plummeting over the side and onto the asphalt.

"I'm...kinda stuck up here." For all Leo's planning and Foil's assistance, not one of them, not even she, had considered how the fuck she was going to get herself *off* the Rex. Bunch of idiots.

The chimp in the road sat down and crossed its legs. It shrugged at her, cocked its head, then started waggling its hands in front of its face, as if trying to shoo away a swarm of bothersome insects.

"Do you understand me?"

The chimp shook his head.

All the other apes in attendance began screeching. Dot thought it sounded like some kind of bastardized version of laughter.

"I'm funny, huh?"

The chimp nodded.

"So you *do* understand me?"

The chimp shook his head. More shrieking laughter.

"I would like to talk to whoever's in charge, if that's possible." She felt like a true ass talking to a fucking monkey...ape...chimp...*whatever* about who was in charge. But it wasn't anymore farfetched than speaking to dinosaurs, so she went with it. "Please," she added for diplomacy.

The chimp in the street leaped to his feet and began flapping his arms. He only stopped momentarily to point to the sky before he returned to the flapping. He continued like this until Dot thought she understood.

"Fly? You wanna fly?"

The chimp jerked his head up and down purposefully. The crowd screeched their response, whatever that was.

"Well..." she thought about her options. She was faced with more than a hundred apes in the suburbs on God-Knew-Where Street, at God-Knew-When o' clock––apes who couldn't engage in conversation but who also understood her. Seemingly. She had no fucking clue what was going on, but she went with it all the same. "Let's see what we can work out."

CHAPTER 8

To Infinity and Beyond!

It wasn't lost on Dot that her new friend's request to help the apes take to the air may have been part of their plan to get the drop on her...friends. Was that what they were? Friends? Co-workers? Randos she'd decided to hang out with 'cause it beat being alone? *Whatever.* Point was, the chimp might have been playing her.

She glanced around either side of Sue. To say there were hundreds of apes surrounding her would have been an understatement. There were definitely more than Leo had said. Regardless, the primates didn't need to sneak up on the humans; they had the numbers to easily overrun them.

What's their plan, then?

She caught a group of apes eyeing her two-legged steed suspiciously. One of them had a stick and looked like he wanted to poke the T-Rex with it.

That won't end well.

And that was when it hit her. The giant fuzzballs were going to attack the dinosaurs. The witch. Dot could get behind that. Maybe if they killed the remaining wicked bitch, she'd finally wake up from this hellacious dream and find herself back in her uncomfortable, twin-size bed.

Problem was, she had no idea how to get the apes into the air. Even if she found a working airplane, who was going to fly it? Certainly not her. *The apes?* Wouldn't that be something to see––flying fucking monkeys. And what were the odds that any of the survivors back at camp knew how to pilot a plane?

Slim to fuck-none most likely.

The chimp who'd made the request didn't appear to be concerned. Maybe he had a plan.

Right. A chimp with a plan. I must be losing it.

Stranger still, the de facto leader cocked his head to the side like a dog hearing its name called.

Did he hear me?

Was he reading her mind? Had she been right all along: did the shoes connect her to the apes like they did to the dinos? Victoria was going to lose her shit when Dot told her about this most recent insanity. That was, if the chimp wasn't just messing with her, which was a distinct possibility.

As Dot pictured the young woman's face, a face she was surprised to find she missed already, a new dilemma arose––and no, it wasn't a newfound interest in chicks. In her previous life, she'd dated equal amounts of men and women. Of course, since her previous life was smack in the middle of Nowheresville, Kansas, what that amounted to was a grand total of one man and one woman. No; the problem was, she needed to pee, badly. Eye-floatingly badly. Which meant she'd have to figure out a way to get off Sue, and then find another way to climb back up when she was done. Cringing and biting her lower lip, she scanned the area. *Nada.* Nothing tall enough for her to use as a step.

Sue must have sensed Dot's anxiousness, because the great beast gave a little whine and slumped to the street, lowering her back as far as she could without rolling over. The lead chimp cocked his head in the other direction, apparently surprised to see an apex predator lying prone on the ground.

Under normal circumstances, jumping off from that height wouldn't have bothered Dot. But after spraining her ankle when she'd jumped into Sue's pen the night before, there was a good chance any fall would hurt like a bitch.

"Any help here?" Dot waved at the chimp, trying to draw his attention.

The chimp shook his head and laughed.

Dot frowned. "Look, I don't have time for your stupid games. I need to pee. As in right this fucking minute. So, unless you want a pissed-on, pissed-off T-Rex running loose around your little camp here, I suggest you help me down."

The chimp squawked, or maybe squealed––it was some sort of high-pitched screech at any rate––then raised his arm and lowered it slowly back to his lap. A number of apes lumbered toward Dot. The first three rolled into balls and crouched shoulder-to-shoulder against Sue's flank. The next two climbed up on top of the first and positioned themselves the same way. The last ape scaled the first two levels and rolled himself into the top step. They'd formed a Donkey Kong Junior pyramid.

"Huh." Dot said.

Should have had Leo and Crow do that back at the base. Demeaning bastards.

Dot swung her left leg around the saddle and put a bit of pressure onto the top ape's back, keeping her right foot in the stirrup and both hands on the grip. Finding the furry structure sturdy, she lowered herself off the saddle and climbed down.

"Thanks. Bum leg." Dot looked at the chimp and waggled her injured foot at him like she was doing the Hokey-Pokey. She refrained from turning herself around.

The chimp slapped an almost disproportionately large hand over his face, then trudged back toward the house he'd appeared from. Dot followed, tiptoeing between the apes that had surrounded her and Sue, half expecting one or all of them to pounce.

Shit. Sue.

She paused and twisted toward the dino. "You be good, Sue," she said. "Don't eat anyone while I'm gone."

Sue pushed a long breath past her giant flapping lips and closed her eyes.

Did she just sigh at me?

Sue rolled her eyes. Dot had to laugh. What else could she do? She added a moody T-Rex to the ever-growing list of absurdities she'd seen and went to check the house into which the chimp had disappeared.

It was a wreck. What furniture remained had been flipped over and tossed against a wall. Large chunks of carpet had been ripped away, and broken tableware and knick-knacks converged in every corner. Surprisingly, most of the framed pictures and paintings still hung on the walls. Of course, every one of them had been desecrated with feces.

Nice, guys. Way to live up to the stereotype.

Dot's new chimp-friend, whom she'd decided to call Fred––'cause why not? ––led her down a dark hallway to the bathroom. The stench hit her before she passed through the doorway. Shit. An assload, by the looks of it. The damn dirty apes had used every surface *but* the toilet to defecate on.

Fred smiled, patted Dot on the back, then waddled back down the corridor.

"Yeah. Thanks."

Pinching her nose between her thumb and forefinger, Dot stepped into the bathroom and elbowed the door closed. She used the tip of her shoe to raise the toilet lid and peeked in. Unbelievably, the water in the bowl was clear. It didn't look like anyone had used it since the water had been shut off. The same could not be said of the room as a whole. The toilet seat looked clean enough, but why chance it? She popped a squat over the porcelain, hovering inches above the plastic ring, and did her business.

Instinctively, she reached for the tissue paper. It looked like the entire roll had been used and then re-rolled onto the cardboard tube. She decided to pass on using it.

UTI here I come.

When she was finished and got back to her feet, something slammed into the roof near her location. It hit hard and then rolled down the slope. A couple seconds later, a second crash shook the house.

That sounded like something came through the ceiling.

Jumping out of the bathroom and walking down the hall as fast as her injured leg allowed, Dot screeched to a halt as she rounded the corner to the living room. Fred was standing over a giant ape lying on the floor. A column of sunlight, similar to a spotlight in a stage play, haloed the poor creature and illuminated a puddle of blood forming around his head and shoulders. Fred was pounding on the dead ape's chest, screaming something Dot was glad she couldn't understand.

How did this happen?

A shadow passed over the hole in the roof, plunging the room in darkness for a moment. Fred dropped to his knees, cowering next to the slain primate. Dot jerked her head up as an unidentifiable shape zipped out of view. Whatever it was, it was big.

"What's going on?" Dot said.

Fred looked up, trembling with fear.

The house shook again––a rumble that knocked dust from the ceiling and shook what picture frames still hung on the walls. But the house hadn't been struck again. It felt and sounded more like an earthquake, and Dot was pretty sure she knew what sound would follow.

Oh no...

Sue's thunderous roar sent Fred back to the floor, the chimp's too-large hands pressed tight against his ears.

Girl, what did you do?

Dot threw open the front door. The scene on the other side was like something out of a Syfy Channel original movie. Broken bodies covered in fur and blood littered the street. Sue stood in the center of it all, screaming at the sky, as howling monkeys rained down all around her.

A flurry of shadows traced the ground, crisscrossing each other and swooping in every direction. Pterodactyls. Flying dinosaurs.

Except, that's not right…

Dot still couldn't remember much of what she should've learned about the Jurassic Period during her school years, but something about the ones hovering overhead stuck out. They weren't technically called Pterodactyls, or the majority of them weren't. Nor were they actually dinosaurs. *Flying lizards,* Dot's teacher had said. Though why that disqualified the winged creatures from being classified as dinosaurs, Dot had no idea. She didn't much care, either.

For each monster that disappeared into the tree line, another appeared, the primate payload it held squirming to free itself from the lizard's talons. *Where were they getting all the apes from?* Had the winged beasts taken them from the stronghold Leo had mentioned? Was that why the apes had moved?

Is that why Fred wanted to fly? To rescue his brothers and sisters?

A spark of adrenaline ignited Dot's blood. She could feel her cheeks flushing; her skin heating up. She needed to do something. One of the Pterodactyls swooped at Sue, its razor talons poised to strike the Rex's face. Sue moved with a grace Dot wouldn't have expected. She feinted to the right then lunged at the brazen creature. The flying lizard squealed as Sue's teeth sank into its lower torso. Sue shook her head like a dog with a toy clenched in its jaw, blood from the lizard spraying this way and that. Then she launched the wounded animal into the trees.

A loud snap followed.

"Sue!" Dot yelled, hobbling into the yard. When the great beast turned, Dot broke into a one-legged run, putting minimal weight on her injured ankle. She leaped onto the back of one of the deceased apes and vaulted toward the saddle on Sue's back. Sue dipped to meet her in the middle.

Dot caught the saddle's grip with her left hand. She sighed with relief and clambered up the dino's flank. She'd just swung her foot into the stirrup when a jolt of searing pain spread across her shoulders. Everything went white and gravity's pull increased dramatically.

When her vision returned, Dot was eye-level with the treetops. One of the Pterodactyls had plucked her off Sue's hide. Its talons dug into her flesh. Blood oozed from the wounds to darken her shirt. The pain was exceptional.

She grabbed the creature's tiny legs and used what strength she had to pull herself up and relieve some of the pressure from her shoulders.

Sue roared, her eyes locked on Dot.

It's not your fault, girl. I should have been paying attention.

Then it hit her. She hadn't even tried to command the 'dactyls. Knowing they weren't technically dinos, she'd figured it wouldn't work. But it seemed like the shoes had allowed her to communicate with Fred, so maybe it didn't matter. Maybe the slippers let her control *all* the transformed animals.

Dot screamed, "Let me go!"

The last syllable left her mouth before the likely consequence of her word choice dawned on her. The 'dactyl released her, and she plummeted into the trees.

She heard another thunderous roar, seconds before the first branch snapped against her back, and the world faded away.

CHAPTER 9

Who's THAT Bitch?

Back in her version of the world, Dot had been a huge fan of RuPaul's *Drag Race*, so when her eyes fluttered open, and she saw a garishly painted face floating above a neck with a prominent Adam's apple, Dot thought she might be dreaming of her favorite show.

"Good morning, my pretty," said the face. Blue tilted ovals were painted around the eyes, while the cheeks were bright red. The foundation wasn't really white but close, which was in contrast to the deep melanin of the rest of their exposed skin. Atop a bright green beehive of hair sat a tiny black witch's hat, no bigger than a 5oz can of tomato juice.

The apparent drag queen seemed to levitate away, and it took Dot a second to realize that they'd been kneeling beside her and had simply risen to standing. They wore a black half-tank, on top of which was a black half-jacket made of leather, with what seemed to be jade jewels for buttons. Across the front of the tank were two words, partially cut off by the flaps of the jacket: -AT BIT-. Dot didn't need to be a Rhodes scholar to know what the missing letters must have been. Peeking from the bustline of the tank were two beige silicone pads that didn't quite match the queen's brown skin, giving the appearance of an A-cup chest. Their knee-length hoop skirt was also jade, with white fringe accents; tank and skirt together framed perfectly chiseled six-pack abs. From their wrist dangled a set of keys that tinkled lightly together.

"Who the fuck are you?" Dot said, her voice more groan than speech.

"Me? Oh, I'm nobody. It's you who're interesting." The queen squinted and glared. "Tell me, pretty, who are *you*, and why do you have on my sister's shoes?"

Dot was on her back, so she sat up to get a better look at the shoes she wore. She shrugged, as if she had no idea where the paw-protectors had come from.

"You can at least tell me if my sister has moved on," they said, their voice soft and friendly, belying the seething hatred in their brown, almost black eyes. The queen smoldered with a tangible anger. Dot could feel it coming off them in waves, like sunbaked asphalt.

"If you mean, is the bitch who was wearing these shoes when I dropped a dumpster on her head still alive, then I'm gonna have to answer in the negative. She's deader than dirt and twice as flat."

Dot did not expect the smile that stretched across the extraordinarily made-up face. The smile did not reach the eyes, though, lending an eerie quality to the queen's countenance. Dot wasn't frightened by much—not on sight, anyway; actions scared her far more than stares and words—but this bitch sent ice through her veins.

"You killed her." It wasn't a question. "I loved her, you know. You may be as cold and callous as you wish, but you should know that I intend to return the favor to everyone you love."

"If this place is real, then from what I gather, everyone I love is already dead, and you and your bitch sister killed them first. So let's say I proactively returned the favor before I was even informed of what you did."

"If this place is real? Now there's a curiosity, pretty. Why wouldn't you think this place is real?"

Dot dusted herself off and got to her feet with more than a modicum of effort. Her neck and back ached, likely due to the fall she'd taken after idiotically making the pterodactyl drop her into the woods, wherein she now stood. The ankle she'd sprained earlier throbbed with fresh agony. She lurched with pain but managed to stay on her feet. The rest of her body felt like a pin cushion, as if she were having acupuncture done by a person with very shaky hands. She rolled her neck and her cervical vertebrae crackled like kindling.

Dot said, "Oh, you know. Dinosaurs that used to be dogs. Cats turned into fuckin' apes. *You.*"

"Me?"

"Yes, *you.*"

"What's so out of place and unrealistic about me, pretty?"

Dot glanced at the tiny witch's hat perched atop that column of neon green hair. "Witches, you shit. You know what I mean."

"Ah," they said with a sigh. "I'm no witch. I'm a wicked bitch, for sure, but I'm no witch. Not in the way you think of witches, at any rate. Witches don't exist. Magic, on the other hand..."

Dot laughed, hard, in their face. She made a sweeping gesture with her hands. "None of this existing makes any sense, but here we are. I'd think I was dreaming, but I just woke up. If I *am* dreaming, this is some *Inception*-level nonsense."

"I liked that movie. Four outta five, would recommend," said the queen.

Dot blinked. "You gotta be fuckin' kidding me right now."

"No, no, I enjoyed it, truly."

"That's not what I meant," Dot said under her breath. "Listen, I got shit to do, and I have a T-Rex named Sue who's probably looking for me, so... peace." Dot threw up two fingers and turned to leave.

"You named my sister's child *Sue*? Are you *mental*?"

Dot shrugged. "Better than Glenda, am I right?"

"I should break you over my knee like a twig, pretty. I should throw you into the sky and let you fall to your death. I should have my friend gobble you up and shit you out on a pile of your friends' bones."

"I'm gonna kill you," Dot promised.

"Not if I kill you first."

It was at this point that Dot stopped thinking of them as "the queen" and went straight for "the Wicked Bitch." Proper noun. Capitalized.

"But I don't think I will. Not yet anyway. You'll come in handy, I'm sure. Bait. You'll be bait for your friends, I think. They'll come to your rescue, and I will end them all. Then we can finally live in peace, without the constant threat of *men* encroaching on our land." The smile on the painted face was a true horror show.

"You won't take me alive," Dot said through gritted teeth.

"You don't have a choice in the matter, my pretty."

Something hit her from behind. She shot forward and hit the ground, forehead first. Her vision swam out of focus then faded altogether.

Before she lost consciousness, Dot thought she heard the Bitch say, "Good boy."

§ § §

Dot surfaced from the void into absolute wakefulness. She felt so *alive*. Her pulse beat steady and strong in her ears, and her mind held a clarity unlike she'd ever known. This wasn't like waking. This was like being shocked back to consciousness after stepping over the edge into the afterlife.

Clear!

She was in a cage: a two-by-four frame wrapped in chicken wire. There was no gate or door that she could see, and she figured the prison had been erected over her while she'd slept, or whatever you'd call the state she had been in before coming to. All around the cage walked dinosaurs of varying shapes and sizes. Dot was no anthropologist—if that was even the right term for what she'd need to be to identify them —so she couldn't place any specific species, but she did know a triceratops and brontosaurus when she saw one, and there were a few of those mixed in with other breeds she was unfamiliar with. The largest of the beasts were at the edges of the mixed herd, looming as tall as skyscrapers, while the smaller beasts roamed the grounds in segregated packs of their own kind. Omnivores and carnivores and herbivores alike existed peaceably among one another. Every one of them seemed amiable; subdued, no doubt, by the Bitch's shoes.

Across from Dot sat another cage of wood and wire, wherein slept the wheezing form of Tutu. She'd forgotten all about her little friend. The dino-doggo kicked its legs in rapid jerks, almost certainly chasing prey in its dreams.

Dot clicked her tongue. Tutu shot upright, as if he'd been awaiting her call the entire time. He loosed a low whine that reminded her of a wolf's howl, or perhaps the fading whistle of a tea kettle removed from a burner.

"Hey, boy," Dot said in a croak. She cleared her throat and repeated herself. "Hey, boy. You okay?"

The feathery raptor nuzzled the wire of its cage and sang a melodious tune in response. He looked as sad as a turkey-sized, feathered lizard could look, Dot figured. A voice, distant, at the back of her mind, told her that Tutu knew cages all too well. He'd been in them before, and being returned to one was akin to being abandoned on church steps by your parents.

Seeing him in that state broke her heart.

"I'm sorry I got us into this mess."

Tutu seemed to nod in forgiveness. His mournful song changed into a screeching yap.

"Can you get out?"

For the next few minutes, Dot watched the tiny bird-like doggo try his best to escape. He scratched and dug at the earth but made little progress; then pecked at the wire, trying to pull it apart, but to no avail. Finally, he sat back on his haunches, looking for all the world like a pet denied a promised treat.

Dot expelled a lengthy breath. "You did good. This ain't on you. It's on me. I'll get us out of this...somehow."

She remembered the walkie in her backpack at the same moment she realized the pack was missing. The Bitch must have confiscated it. She and Tutu were on their own.

Dot sat down in the grass in one corner of her prison and watched the dinosaurs around her mill about—some chomping grass, while others rubbed against each other with obvious affection. In one group, a two-legged dino mounted another and began pumping away. Soon enough, many of the others joined in, with complete disregard for gender and species.

"Great," Dot said aloud, "I'm in the middle of a fuckin' Jurassic orgy. How wonderful."

The sun dropped behind the trees in the distance, and Dot was left in utter darkness before the moon made its appearance. The fingernail-sliver rose, softly illuminating the now sleeping herd of dinosaurs who had by then fucked themselves into comas. The air reeked of their lovemaking.

Somewhere in the night, a cackle exploded into life. Dot had no doubt that the laughter came from the Wicked Bitch, although there was no way to know for sure. Of one thing she was certain, though: there were no other humans here. Just her and the Bitch. And Dot promised herself that, even if it was the last thing she did, she'd have that drag queen's head on a platter, so help her God.

She didn't sleep that night, for fear that she'd wake up outside of this new world and be denied her revenge.

"Victoria," Dot said, as the sickle moon crossed the sky, "be careful. Please, *please*, be careful."

CHAPTER 10

Finagle's Law

Several years ago...

"You sure this is okay?" Chastity Holmes sat at the edge of her bed, crisscross applesauce, her eyes glued to her bedroom door and the crucifix hanging dead center above it. Her blond hair was draped around her shoulders, hands clasped over her legs. "Mama says giving in to such temptation is no better than fornicating with the devil himself."

"What a bunch of hogwash."

Victoria knelt in front of the bed, her chin tucked between Chastity's overlapping, sun-kissed ankles, arms wrapped around the other girl's backside. "She's just jealous cause she knows no woman on the planet would want to touch her love cave."

"Victoria!" Chastity slapped a hand over her mouth, then *yipped*, startled at the volume of her own voice. "That's horrible."

"Please, it's true. How a troll like her gave birth to such a beautiful girl, I'll never figure. You sure you weren't adopted? Kidnapped, maybe? Stolen from some hapless parents crossing her bridge without paying the toll?"

Smiling, Chastity finally met Victoria's eyes. She leaned in and kissed her, ever so gently, on the lips. Then, her cheeks pink with embarrassment, she pulled away and returned to her unblinking observation of the door.

"She's not coming in." Victoria ran a finger along Chastity's waistband, her feathery touch drawing the fine hairs on the girl's back like a magnet. At the top of the bed Chuckles, Chastity's black and white Australian Shepherd, whined. Probably chasing a squirrel in his dreams.

Chastity trembled at Victoria's touch. "How do you know that?"

Chuckles' eyes popped open. The pup crossed the bed and jumped down, out of view.

"Because the universe doesn't hate me that much," Victoria said, then kissed Chastity's calf.

"What? That's it?" Leaning back, Chastity propped herself up on her elbows. "You're going to risk her disowning me, or worse, killing us both, on your faith in the universe?"

"Yup." Victoria slid her hand down and squeezed Chastity's ass.

Chastity *yipped* again, jumping back, out of Victoria's grasp. "You're terrible."

"Sometimes."

The nervous girl fell flat on the bed, arms sprawled out to the sides. Then she screamed. It was a bloodcurdling howl, sending goosebumps up and down Victoria's arms. A chill surged across her body. Chastity cried out again.

Victoria looked up.

A creature hunched over the far side of the bed, all teeth and scales and... *feathers?* Its wicked mouth was embedded in Chastity's stomach, chewing voraciously, digging deeper. It tore a rope of intestines from Chastity's abdomen and chomped on it until blood and shit oozed from the torn innards. The girl's screams subsided as she succumbed to the pain. Victoria's harried screams took their place.

The hell is that?!?

Collecting herself, Victoria said, "Fuck the universe," under her breath and pushed to her feet.

While the monster was focused on chewing its meal, she crept toward the door. Chuckles was nowhere to be found. There wasn't even a stray piece of fur to signal his existence before being eaten by the vicious thing devouring Chastity. The creature raised its head. An unchewed length of bloody intestine dropped from its mouth.

It reared back, then sank its teeth into Chastity's neck.

Victoria screamed again.

With its teeth clenched around Chastity's neck and shoulder, the monster hoisted her off the bed and shook her like a ragdoll. Blood squirted, splattering the walls, the ceiling, and the bedspread Chastity's grandmother had quilted for her by hand. It tossed the girl across the room. Her limp corpse slammed into the desk on the far wall, sending a laptop and a stack of papers careening to the floor. The creature turned toward Victoria and roared.

Flecks of blood sprinkled Victoria's face and chest. Her legs were suddenly warm––she'd peed herself. Instinct kicked in. She flung the door open, spun through the entryway, then slammed the door shut. Heavy footfalls echoed toward her from the other side. She bolted down the hallway, heartbeat thundering, and bounced off Chastity's mom as they both rounded the corner.

"Wha––" the woman yelped as they collided and ricocheted off opposite walls.

Using her hands to spring off the gaudy, black-and-white Fleurs-de-lis wallpaper, Victoria shouldered past the much larger woman and sprinted for the front door.

What the fuck is going on?

Something exploded behind her. Chastity's bedroom door. The creature was still coming.

Mrs. Holmes screamed. Her cries were fearful at first, but they soon became something else. They raised an octave––the sound of pure agony. Wet, gnashing sounds faded as Victoria continued her escape.

She reached the door as the noises from the hallway ceased altogether. She leaped outside and ran for her mom's forest-green Taurus, which was parked in the driveway behind Chastity's white Corolla. When she was halfway to her car, she skidded to a halt. Screams filled the air, some muffled within the nearby houses, some clear as a newborn's innocence. The monsters were everywhere: attacking people on the street, bursting out of houses, fighting with each other over their prey.

Not monsters. Dinosaurs.

Dinosaurs of every shape, size, and color.

A four-foot creature on two legs chased a squealing man into the street, where it leaped and tackled him to the asphalt. It tore at the back of the man's neck like a ravenous dog chomping at its food bowl.

A trio of beasts, all small and feathered, fell upon a chubby woman in a bathrobe in her front yard. One of the creatures tore at the curlers in her hair, while another gnawed at her ankle. The last one went for her throat.

A massive sound, like the Earth itself expelling a held breath, rumbled through the ground as something long and tall and wide rose on the horizon. The brontosaurus extended its neck and lowed, not unlike a cow mooing, before lumbering off in the opposite direction.

Above, screeching birds circled.

No. Not birds. These things were much bigger; triangular and bat-like, but ten times the size of the nocturnal mammals.

A pair of apes swung down the middle of the road, chasing what looked like a baby triceratops. The smaller, three-horned thing squealed like a pig as it ran, its pursuers shrieking excitedly in their primate voices.

What the hell is happening?

A roar less than fifty feet away jolted Victoria out of her stupor. She beelined for the rear, driver side door, dove in, and pulled the door closed.

She scurried into the floorboards between the seats. Curled up in the fetal position, she lay there for who knows how long. Crying. Praying.

Eventually, she passed out.

§ § §

"Hey, what are you doing? Wake up." The voice was familiar, but it sounded far away, across a gulf as wide as Victoria's fear. "Victoria, wake up!"

Victor?

Victoria's eyes snapped open. She was slumped beside the campfire, the earth cold beneath her. Victor towered above her head. "What's going on?" she said.

"You fell asleep is what's going on. What the hell?" The sun was on his back, so she couldn't see his eyes, but she could feel her brother's glare boring into her forehead. He wouldn't meet her gaze. His lack of self-confidence kept him from focusing on anyone else's eyes. He tended to stare at chests instead, which had gotten him in trouble with many women back before the world moved on. There was nothing perverted about this tendency, only a simple unwillingness to meet their eyes. He'd sought therapy for his social awkwardness, but had managed only two visits before everything went to shit.

Victoria rolled to her knees. "So I did. Had a dream, too."

Placing his hand on his hips, he said, "This isn't funny, sis. You were supposed to be watching the south ridge."

"We came up the south ridge. There's nothing there."

"That's not the point."

Victoria got to her feet and brushed herself off. "Then what *is* the point, Vic?"

"If Leo finds out, if he thinks you can't be trusted to follow orders, he's not going to let you leave the compound. Can you imagine being stuck there all the time?"

She huffed, crossed her arms over her chest, and shook her head. "You know, the only person I've felt any sort of connection with since all this bullshit started just wandered into the woods, riding on the back of a fucking T-Rex to talk some monkeys into not killing us."

"They're apes, not mon—"

"I don't fuckin' *care*, Vic. Dot's trying to save our skins. I probably won't ever see her again, so I don't give a good God damn what––"

The walkie dangling from Victor's hip squawked. "Uh, guys."

It was Crow.

Victor fumbled with the carabiner, detached it, and then brought the handheld to his lips. He pushed talk. "What is it, Crow?" he said. "What do you see?"

"It's Dot..."

The pause that followed stretched out into eternity. Tears welled behind Victoria's eyes; a breath caught in her chest. Her legs went numb, knees trembling.

"Unless our girl can fly, I don't reckon she's gonna to make it," Crow continued. "I think she's gone, y'all."

Victoria fell to her knees, sobbing into her hands.

CHAPTER 11

A New Hope?

Victor found the crash site. After all, he'd been the one who'd pinpointed the exact landing spot of Dot's dumpster. He never revealed how he'd hit the mark so perfectly, but Victoria knew her brother was a smart dude. Always had been. That's why they'd survived as long as they had: his brains, and her tenacity.

Victoria recalled how she'd felt, seeing Dot climbing from the dumpster: a strange mixture of attraction and terror. *Who was this woman, and was she dangerous?* Somehow the threat of danger had only served to heighten Victoria's attraction. Yet there was something beyond Dot's mystique that had drawn Victoria in. The simplest answer was surface level: Dot was fucking hot. The more complicated answer was: Victoria was lonely. It was her loneliness that concerned her. Were her burgeoning feelings for Dot based solely on the possibility that she might have a chance with the other woman, or was Victoria truly falling in love? Could you even fall in love so quicky? Love at first sight tended to boil down to lust more than honest affection; Victoria was well aware of that. But she couldn't put a finger on

Dot's extra *something*ness. Hell, perhaps it was only the fact that Dot could be dangerous.

All girls have a bad boy phase, her mother had told her, back before the world went Jurassic. Victoria assumed the same could be said of girls who loved girls as well. She'd spent so much of her life in hiding that she'd grown accustomed to the idea that she might die alone. After the world went to shit, and her options were further limited, that reasoning only intensified. That was, until Dot fell from the heavens into her lap, like some kind of called-upon angel. She thanked whatever higher power had seen fit to insert Dot into her life, though. Amen, and thank you...*whoever*!

The crew of survivors had been on the move for over four hours by the time Victor led them to the relevant place in the woods. Dot's downward trajectory was clearly marked by a finger of light pouring through the treetops. It was as if a meteor had crashed through the canopy, so perfectly circular was the tunnel through the branches. Broken limbs littered the area, splintered like snapped popsicle sticks– aside from a vaguely human-shaped spot where Dot had hit the ground. Victoria thought it looked a bit like those old Warner Bros. cartoons: when Bugs runs through a wall, leaving a rabbit-eared outline in his wake.

"This is definitely it," Leo said. He knelt by the outline and studied it a moment, as if he could discern in which direction Dot had moved, or been taken, simply by poking at the snapped detritus scattered about the area. Shit, maybe he *could* track Dot like that; Victoria honestly didn't know if Leo was capable of such feats. The man was ex-military, so...maybe? Well, he was ex-military only in the sense that there was no military left, but she had no doubt that if any branch of the military still existed, Leo would be a part of it. Perhaps their crew of survivors *was* Leo's military.

Sure. Why not?

"I reckon they moved the body," Crow said. He shouldered his rifle and took a knee beside his leader. "Huh..."

"What? Speak up," Leo said.

"Ain't no blood, boss." Crow dusted his hands and rose again to his full height.

"He's right!" Victoria shrieked. She forced herself to calm down before saying. "I mean, it's no guarantee she's *alive*. She could have internal injuries. Oh shit, that would be horrible. What if she's bleeding internally? Fuck. Goddamn it. Is she all right?"

"Hey," Victor said, placing a calming hand on her should, "slow down, sis."

Victoria shrugged him off. "I'm worried. I have every *right* to be worried. She's my...She's *our* only hope, asshole."

Crow chuckled. "Okay, Obi Wan."

"It was *Leia* who said that, you righteous fuckwit," Victoria said.

Crow put his hands up. "Calm down, sweet cheeks, I was just playin.'"

"Play with your tiny ass cock and leave me alone. Shit! It's like you don't even *care* what happened to her!"

"And why you care so goddamn much, huh?" Crow asked. There was a suspicious cast to the gaze he'd set on her. It reminded her of how her mother looked when she asked why Victoria never talked about boys. *Because I'm gay, Mom, that's why.* Of course, Victoria had never uttered those words, but that didn't mean she hadn't wanted to, and with her whole soul.

"*Because*, you inbred hillbilly, she's the only chance we got here. Am I fuckin' *wrong*?"

"You're right," Leo said as he stood and stretched his back. "Dot's important. And I don't think she's dead."

"Really?" Victoria and Crow asked in tandem. Crow glanced her way, and she stuck out her tongue at him.

Jinx. You owe me a coke, cocksucker.

"I'd like to think my plan's worked," Leo said.

"What plan?" said Victoria.

"Why do you think I let her go alone, Vicky?"

"Don't call me that. You know I can't stand—"

"Sorry. *Victoria*, why do you think I let her go alone? This—" he gestured around him like Christ rotating on a cross, "—is *exactly* what I was hoping for. Now we can follow her trail to wherever they took her and—"

"*You used her as fuckin' bait*?" Victoria screamed. She took two long strides towards Leo and decked him in the jaw. His head snapped to the right, but he didn't go down. Her father had always told her, "If you swing at someone, you might not get a chance at another one, so make sure you put them on their ass with the first one, ya dig?" She'd given it all she had, on God she had, but all that happened was a fresh hell brewing in her right fist. She crossed her arms, tucking her throbbing knuckles into her armpit, and bit down on her lip in order to keep from crying out in pain. She could only hope she hadn't broken her fucking hand.

Leo placed a finger to the corner of his mouth, as if checking for blood, before giving Victoria a smile. "Nice punch."

"Fuck you." She almost choked on a sob that was equal parts agony and anger. "You're a monster, using her like that. I should fuckin' kill you."

"We had no other choice. Like you said, Vicky—sorry, *Victoria*—Dot's our only chance here."

"And you probably fuckin' murdered her for her trouble!" Victoria raged.

"Oh, I have no doubt she's alive, girl. She's a tough bitch."

"I'll show you a tough bitch, you arrogant—"

"Victoria." There was Victor's hand again. She spun on her brother, grabbed one of his shoulders in each hand, and kneed him in the balls. He went down whining like a spent bottle rocket.

"*I said don't fuckin' touch me!*"

"If you'll do that to family, remind me never to piss you the fuck off. Jaysus." Crow got to chuckling again, but Victoria noticed with more than a modicum of fright that his palm was now resting on his sidearm and the leather strap had been pulled away. Would he have shot her, had she gone any further than kneeing Victor? If she'd jumped her brother, would Crow have ended her? She couldn't tell herself *no* with any amount of certainty. But she also refused to be scared into submission, much less be forced to calm down by a swinging-dick asshole like Crow.

"Too late, motherfucker." Victoria reeled to face Leo again. "And *you*, you arrogant puddle of semen, had better hope she's still alive, 'cause if she isn't, I'm gonna rain hell down on your balls until they're fuckin' stardust."

Leo's smile widened. "That's the spirit. Onward, shall we?"

§ § §

They came across the massacre a few minutes later. Ape corpses were scattered and splattered about the suburban street and the driveways of homes, though not one body littered the grass of any of the front yards. Victoria didn't have to be a rocket scientist to figure out they'd been dropped from an insane height; nor did she think that their having been dropped on only hard surfaces was an accident.

"What the hell happened here?" Foil asked from inside his power armor.

"It's a slaughterhouse," Crow said.

"Obviously, dumbass," Foil muttered.

"Jesus Christ," Victor whined, still clutching his balls. Victoria was surprised he could even walk, given how hard she'd kneed him. His nuts would be touching his tonsils for a week or more; she was sure of it.

Leo cleared his throat. "'Dactyls is my guess, or something like 'em."

"Under the witch's control, no doubt, too." Crow nodded once in a quick up and down motion. Victoria heard his neck crack. Crow reached for his nape and massaged it. "I'm stiffening up, boss. Gonna have to bed down for the night. My C-3 is actin' a right bastard."

"Is that such a good idea?" Victoria asked. She wanted to find Dot, now. Not later. So as not to add further fuel to the fire of their suspicions she added, "It doesn't seem safe here."

Leo sighed, "You're probably right." He directed the next bit at Crow: "You're just gonna have to suffer. I wanna cover as much ground as possible."

"Y'all can suck the salt off my sweaty nuts. I ain't gonna be no good to nobody if I can't move my goddamn neck, Leo."

"You'll be fine."

"You say that now, but just wait until you need me to shoot something and I can't aim down-sights because I got an elephant-sized crick in my neck."

"You'll. Be. Fine," Leo emphasized.

"*You'll be fine,*" Crow mumbled in a mocking voice.

"Check that tone, soldier."

"*Yessir,*" Crow shouted. He snapped off a sarcastic salute before moving into the carnage slathered all over the suburban street.

Once Crow was out of earshot, Leo asked Victoria, "You okay?"

"Like you care."

"I do, actually. We been together for a long time, girl. Been through shit with you I ain't been through with men in combat. You always hold your own, and I respect that. You think I liked using an innocent girl—"

"She a woman, you shit."

"Fine. You think I liked using an innocent woman as bait? If it'd been a man, I'd have done the same, so's you know. This ain't about her being—"

"I know that. Just...drop it. Okay?"

"I can do that. So, what's your input here? You thinking we should really move on with Crow in the condition he's in? I hate to say it, but he's right. If he's worthless, so are we."

Victoria growled low in her throat. "I don't fuckin' know, Leo." She paused to collect herself. She *would not* cry in front of him. "I just wanna know that she's okay."

Leo extended his arms. "Can I give you a hug?"

"What? Fuck no! Why...why the hell would you wanna hug me?"

Leo shrugged. "Seemed right, I guess."

"Just...just keep your paws to yourself. I'm fine."

"You are *not* fine." Leo glanced to where Crow was toeing the exploded ribs of one unlucky ape where it had splattered across the pavement. Leo said, "She's real pretty, that Dot."

"Yeah. I guess so." She'd had her guard down, what with watching Crow be a heartless asshole.

"You fancy her." It was not a question.

"Well, yeah, she—Wait. What the fuck you getting at?"

"Come on, Vicky." There was her mother's look again; that look that said, "I know you're a sinner, child..."

"Stop calling me that." With that, she left Leo where he stood. She said the rest over her shoulder as she stepped over a mangled ape and into one of the nearest open houses: "Camp for the night for all the fucks I give! Let Crow rest his pussy ass neck, the little bitch!"

She found what had to have been the master bedroom, once upon a when, and sat her tired ass on the moldy mattress. The room was redolent with an animalistic funk, a heavy, musty odor Victoria thought she could see. For a time, she cried softly, until the dam broke and she devolved into an emotional wreck. Still, she kept an ear out, just in case one of her crew stumbled in after her. No one came, though. Not even Victor. She was all alone. Why that should have bothered her so much now, after being alone for so goddamn long, was anyone's guess.

CHAPTER 12

The Ballad of Mr. Cuddles

everal years ago...

Victoria woke in the same position she'd fallen asleep: curled up between the seats of her mother's ugly-ass Taurus. While she'd slept, night had fallen. Her neck hurt like hell.

How long was I out?

She peeked over the backseat, but all she saw was darkness. Closing her eyes, she nearly strained a muscle in her jaw, trying to hear the world outside the car. There was the muffled chittering of night things, and the lonesome whine of something in the distance.

The screams had died out--most likely with the people who'd been doing the screaming. She wanted to get out, to look for survivors or someone to help her, but she'd seen enough movies to know you never go outside when things get quiet. A false sense of security will get you killed quicker than clear and present danger.

Feeling safe enough to move about inside the vehicle, Victoria climbed over the armrest and dropped into the driver's seat. She fished the keys out of her purse--thankfully, she'd left her handbag on the passenger seat when she'd gone inside earlier, in case she and Chastity got caught and the need arose for Victoria to bail--and started the car. She reached in again, trying to find her cell phone, and remembered she'd left it on Chastity's bed.

Fuck!

The image of Chastity being hollowed out by that horrible creature flashed before her: ropes of intestines dangling from its chewing mouth; Chastity screaming until she could scream no more.

And the blood. There had been so much *blood.*

The sudden urge to puke overwhelmed her. She pawed at the door handle, frantically trying to pull it open, and got it open a second before she retched onto the driveway.

Something *cawed* in the distance. But it wasn't distant *enough*; and perhaps it wasn't a caw, after all. More like a shrieking, akin to a poorly-oiled gate creaking open.

Victoria looked up, wiping her arm across her mouth, and scanned the trees lining the sidewalk. When she heard the sound again, it was closer. She pulled the door closed, anxiety building as it latched in place with the tiniest *click*. Then, leaving the headlights off, she reversed out of the driveway, bumping over bodies as she went. There was no helping it. Corpses were everywhere. And besides, they were already dead. She wasn't hurting anyone. She coasted down the street, zigzagging around bodies when she could, rolling over them when she couldn't, until she finally left Chastity's neighborhood behind.

What the hell is going on?

No other cars were on the road. No one running, anyway. She travelled through lifeless neighborhoods on her way to the interstate, the eeriness of this land devoid of life not lost on her. It was like the whole world had disappeared while she slept, its silent march into nothingness a portent of her own impending fate. When she turned onto the highway entry ramp, she dared to activate the Taurus' headlights and accelerated. She regretted it immediately. Monsters the size of houses slumbered in the grass alongside the road.

Slapping a hand over her mouth, Victoria tried to stifle the scream pulsating in her throat. She took her foot off the gas, her eyes glued to the creatures as the car slowed to a crawl. The interstate seemed miles and miles away, although the ramp couldn't have been longer than five-hundred-feet.

As she crept along, an eye popped open to her right.

Victoria *yelped* and jammed her foot on the gas. Her back and head slammed into the seat as the car leaped forward.

Oh my God, oh my God, oh my God!

The Taurus blasted onto the highway, veering left then right as Victoria fought to regain control.

After straightening out, she chanced a look in the rearview mirror. Nothing followed. She was alone. All alone in a world that had gone completely insane––and that was putting it mildly. She needed to get home, back to her family. Her dad would know what to do.

The house was dark when Victoria arrived. She pulled into the driveway behind her dad's Silverado and cut the lights and engine.

Where the hell's Victor?

His car wasn't in the driveway. Victoria craned her neck to look out the rear window for Victor's silver Eclipse. It wasn't parked on the street, either.

You better be okay, dumbass. 'Cause I'll kill you if you're not.

She checked all around the Taurus again, scanning for monsters this time. Then, confident she was alone, Victoria opened the door, slipped out, and closed it again, using both hands to keep it from slamming shut and alerting anything murderous to her presence. She double checked her surroundings, then ran for the front door. It was unlocked. Victoria fought every urge to say, *Hello? Anybody home?* as she entered. Her love of scary movies had also taught her that never ended well.

Reflexively, she paused in the foyer, waiting for Mr. Cuddles to charge down the hallway and prance around her ankles, tongue hanging out as he begged for her attention. But the Scottish Terrier was nowhere to be found.

Other than the missing pooch, the only other thing that seemed out of character was the darkness. Her parents usually left a light on, especially if she or Victor weren't home.

Turning left into the living room, she froze, sucked in a breath. A cold burst of adrenaline swirled in her belly, then arced into her chest and arms, like nitrous shooting into an engine. The house's west wall was gone. Well, not gone exactly. There was a giant hole between dad's recliner and the couch. A dinosaur-shaped hole.

Victoria's breathing increased, matching her rapid heartbeat. Silence enveloped her. She clenched her jaw and headed for the bedrooms, beginning to feel lightheaded. Using the wall to keep herself upright as she traversed the corridor, she passed her room, then Victor's, trudging toward her parent's open door.

Her hand trembling, Victoria fumbled for the light switch. The sudden burst of light blinded her. When her vision adjusted, her parent's bed lay before her, the comforter and headboard slathered with blood. The wall behind it looked as if someone had tried renovating with a paintball gun full of red ammo.

No, no, no…

She spun, hand clasped over her mouth, fighting the urge to vomit again. Her legs buckled, and she fell to her knees.

"They can't be gone," she muttered. "They can't be."

She slumped to the floor, the carpet soft on her skin, and sobbed. There weren't any bodies, but with that much blood, she didn't need to see bodies to know what had happened.

When she could cry no more, Victoria pushed up onto her hands and knees and crawled back down the hall. She used Victor's doorknob to get back on her feet, then held her breath as she turned it and let the door creak open.

Hesitant, she reached for the light switch.

Please be okay. I can't be alone. You need to be okay.

She sighed as light filled Victor's room. It hadn't been touched and was blessedly free of ichor. Her room also appeared to be just as she'd left it. Turning the light off and closing the door, she stumbled toward her bed, climbed on top, and buried herself under the covers, clutching Mr. Giggles, her stuffed turtle, as if the soft creature would come alive and try to escape her grasp.

She couldn't be alone right now.

She couldn't.

Could not...

§ § §

Bang!

What the hell was that?

Victoria bolted upright in bed, sweat that had beaded at her brow rolling into her eyes. She swiped the salty liquid from her lids and wiped her fingers dry on her shirt. The summer heat was oppressive, and even sleeping on top of the disgusting blanket hadn't helped keep her cool. She'd taken air conditioning for granted, in her PJ––pre-Jurassic––life.

It was still dark outside, and the others hadn't found her; or if they had, they'd decided to leave her be.

A second *Bang!* rang out, the report closer this time. Jumping off the bed, Victoria ran to the door and bumped head-first into Victor as he entered. She ricocheted off his chest and landed on her ass.

"What the fuck?" she said, getting back to her feet.

Panic was plastered all over Victor's sweaty face. His bottom lip trembled.

"We...we have to go," he said. "Now!" Victor grabbed her wrist and tugged her through the doorway.

"What's going on? Is someone shooting?"

Victoria stumbled over her feet trying to keep up with her brother's pace as he pulled her through the house. When they reached the front porch, she stopped dead, snapping Victor back toward her like a yo-yo.

Her mouth fell open, her stomach somersaulting.

Crow was lying on top of the neighboring house, struggling on the angled roof to get a bead on a Carnotaurus less than thirty yards away. The horned beast trampled Foil and his oversized trash compactor as it charged towards Leo. Somehow, Foil's rig continued to move. The dinosaur hadn't wrecked it. Their courageous leader was fifteen feet behind the prone power armor, backing up in Victor and Victoria's direction.

Oh my g—

Bang!

CHAPTER 13

Oh...Well...

The shot rang out, startling Victoria, though she was already scared shitless. Crow's aim was true, but the Carnotaurus snapped its horned dome at the last second, causing the sniper's bullet to ricochet off the bipedal T-Rex-wannabe's right horn. The beast shook its head in the aftermath of the impact, like a dazed boxer might shake off an opponent's glancing blow.

"Fuck!" Crow roared from his place on the house's roof. Getting to his feet to reposition, he lined up another shot, but before he could squeeze the trigger, he lost his footing and went sliding off the roof like a kid down a Slip 'N Slide. He smashed shoulder-first into the withered front lawn. Victoria heard his collarbone snap from thirty yards away.

"Crow!" she screamed, stuck in the moment, rooted in place by a fear more restricting than being buried in cement.

"Run!" Leo hollered, but she couldn't move.

The Carnotaurus took an unsteady step in reverse, before taking another two stumbling steps forward. It raised its toothy mouth to the sky and bellowed. Victoria covered her ears to protect them from the keening.

"Victoria, come on!" That was Victor, somehow to her right and her left, in front of and behind her, his voice muffled and brilliantly loud all at once. It took her a moment to realize she still had her ears covered.

Several pops sounded, the telltale noise of Leo trying his best to distract the confused dinosaur with shots from his sidearm. Because what else could he be doing? No way Leo would have thought the .45's tiny bullets would have any other effect on the 25-foot-tall creature. She watched in stunned horror as red holes opened on the Carnotaurus' flank, like zits popping of their own accord. Blood black as midnight ran from the miniscule wounds, and Victoria wondered if they bothered the beast any more than a mosquito bite might affect an elephant.

"Goddamn it, Victoria, run!" Leo hollered again as the Carnotaurus regained its composure and sought its next meal.

Three things happened then, in tandem:

Leo dashed to where Crow lay crumpled in the front yard of the house from whose roof he'd fallen.

Foil's power armor cycled and whirred, as the man inside of it struggled to get the thing back on its mechanical feet.

And Victor snatched his sister, pulling her back toward house they'd just fled.

The Carnotaurus ignored Leo and Crow, Foil and his power armor, and set after Victoria and her brother as they rushed across dead grass, up three low concrete steps, and through the decrepit doorway of the bungalow. Although Victoria didn't see the dinosaur crash into the front wall of the house, she sure as hell felt it. The impact of the monstrous beast hitting the building shook the foundation. Victor went careening into a wall, where he bounced off and tilted, dropping to the carpet like a toppled tree.

Victoria, caught off balance by the quake, stumbled and lurched into the kitchen as the foyer collapsed, spewing wood and rubble and dust into the air. She screamed and rolled and went crashing into the kitchen's island, damn near shattering her hip upon impact. She braced herself against the countertop, tried to catch her breath.

The Carnotaurus' foot came through the ceiling in an explosion of framing and drywall. Victoria shrieked, spun, and headed for the first doorway she could see; hoping, praying even, that beyond the door lay salvation. She reached it, grabbed the knob, threw the door open...

...and stepped into a garage that might as well have been a death-row prison cell. Inside the garage sat a brand-new (or what had once *been* a brand-new) Dodge Charger. The paint job was still an immaculate cherry red under a fine layer of dust, but the tires had been eaten away over the years by rodents and no doubt various other pests. Each aluminum rim was ringed with black rubber and white thread, like the fringe on a rodeo cowboy's jacket. She had no hopes that the car would be her escape. Even if she could find the keys, there was no way in Satan's asshole that the battery would have held its charge all this time after the end of the world. Same with the garage door, which she could clearly see was operated by the device dangling from the ceiling above the Charger. No electricity meant there was no way to open the garage door, not unless she used the manual bypass, but she didn't have time for that shit. All this information she parsed in seconds, before diving for the passenger side door of the car and yanking it open.

The interior of the car was a horror show. A desiccated corpse sat behind the driver's seat. Its throat had been ripped out, the ragged flesh like torn paper framing the dull gray of the spinal cord. Aged blood covered everything, the obsidian goop dotting surfaces like shiny beetles and glistening worms frozen in cryogenic stasis. Curled into the footwell of the passenger seat was the shriveled corpse of a small dinosaur, something akin to Dot's little friend Tutu, but half his size. Victoria didn't have to be an anthropologist to figure out what had happened. The owner of the Charger had gone for a ride with their canine companion and had arrived home the moment the world went to shit. The dog had gone full dino, killed its owner, but had found no way to escape the car's interior. No opposable thumbs, no opening the door. Simple as that. Nothing to do but wait and starve to death. You hate to see it.

The Carnotaurus roared as it tore its way into the house proper, and Victoria, without planning to or so much as thinking, dove into the Charger, twisted, and tugged the door closed behind her. She crawled into the backseat, drew her knees to her chest, and began to shake and sob uncontrollably.

Even if she could no longer see the massive creature tearing its way through the bungalow, she could feel it. With every step into and through the house, the creature shook the car on its tireless rims. The screeching cacophony of the Carnotaurus' raging and the grinding of aluminum on the bare concrete floor of the garage was maddening. Victoria covered her ears and screamed at the top of her lungs, hoping that the devil she knew (her own voice) was better than the devil she didn't (the sound of approaching doom).

The wall that separated the kitchen from the garage vanished in a cloud of dust and rubble. The Carnotaurus' massive scaly foot, shin, and knee came into view first, as if it were stepping out from a dense London fog, before the creature retracted it a second later. Through the new gap poked the creature's horned head, and Victoria had a moment of insanity as it struck her just how much the goddamn thing looked like a medieval court jester in one of those funny tricorn hats––minus one corn, of course.

With a sudden thrust, the beast headbutted the side of the Charger. The car rocked on its rims, slid, and slammed into the far wall. The Carnotaurus retreated a few feet, plaster dust and splintered wood raining down in its absence, before ramming the car again. Victoria, screaming and weeping, crammed herself farther into the driver's side of the backseat. She realized with a spike of disconsolate terror that she had nowhere else to go. With the driver's side door flush with the garage wall, and the passenger side doors smashed in by the Carnotaurus' assault, there was no opening any of them. And if she so much as stuck her head out of the space where the windows on the passenger side had once been, the monster would surely pluck her from the car like a gopher from its hidey hole.

She was going to die.

She was going to die in the backseat of a Dodge Charger, smashed to death, like a junkyard wreck in a hydraulic trash compactor.

The creature came again, ramming and crushing with its weaponized skull. The windshield, which had up until this point spiderwebbed but not shattered, finally exploded outward, raining safety glass onto the crumpled hood.

Which was when Victoria saw the door at the rear of the garage. She hadn't seen it before because it had been hidden by a workbench and tool cabinet setup on the back wall. Without considering whether or not her next move was the smartest of ideas, she scrambled over the center console, squeezed between the front seats, and pulled herself onto the dashboard. She crawled out onto the hood, panting and sweating, terror and heat coming off her in waves. Gummy safety glass dug into her sweat-slicked palms and jeaned knees. She slipped at the edge of the hood and nosedived onto the detritus-strewn concrete floor of the crumbling garage.

She didn't look back, nor did she wait to be snatched up. She clambered to her feet and dashed for the door. Instead of fucking with the doorknob, she threw her entire shoulder into the door and, with adrenaline's help, knocked the motherfucker from its hinges. She exploded out into glorious sunlight and fresh air...

...only to find herself in a backyard with a nine-foot privacy fence, every slat topped with wickedly sharp points that would make any vampire huntress horny on main.

"Fuck this whole goddamn motherfucking day!" Victoria shrieked.

"Victoria!"

She snapped around to find where the voice was coming from and saw Victor in the far corner of the backyard. He must've escaped the house through the back door or something. Thank God for that.

He'd dug at the ground around one of the fence slats and had managed to pry one of the boards loose at the bottom. She ran around what looked like an antiquated well, complete with crank and bucket, that had to be decorative in a neighborhood like this, and came to a stuttering halt beside her brother. His hands were cut to shit from working at the fence, and blood cascaded from them in rivulets of thick, ropey red.

"Your hands..." she let her voice trail off.

"Fuck my hands," he panted. "Help me."

All this time, Victoria remained aware of the Carnotaurus' roars as it demolished the house, but she dared not look behind her, not so much as a glance. No, sir, no how. And because of this, she did not see the monster take her brother.

One moment Victor was there, at her side, helping her pull the slat from the fence, ensuring their safe getaway. And then he was gone. She turned to ask him what he was doing, to tell him to get the fuck back here and help her, goddamn it, to stop being a lazy bastard, but he wasn't there.

He'd never be there again.

She craned her neck to gaze up at the Carnotaurus as its jaws worked on her brother. Victor never made a sound. Not a peep. He died quietly, like so much of the world had. Like Victoria's own heart had.

"No!" she shrieked. She rushed the monster and began punching its massive leg, as if she could pummel it into a pile of meat and carnage.

The Carnotaurus leaned to one side and kicked, like Victor used to do if his balls were stuck to his thigh, and Victoria went flying. She crashed through the cute little steepled roof of what she had thought was a decorative well and plummeted down, down, down, into darkness.

The well, it seemed, wasn't so decorative after all.

CHAPTER 14

Cloudbusting with Style

*S*everal years ago...

Victoria's eyes snapped open. *What was that?* Something had pulled her from a deep sleep. At first, she'd thought she'd dreamt the door closing somewhere nearby. But that sort of thing never woke her. Hell, just two nights ago she'd had a pleasant dream about going down on Jennifer Lawrence, only to have her mom and dad walk in. If the near heart attack she'd had that night didn't wake her, nothing would.

She slipped out of the bed and crossed the room to the door. Holding her breath, she placed her ear on the faux-wood and listened. Footsteps in the distance. Faint, but unmistakable. They were too quiet to belong to one of those... things. *Unless they come in Happy Meal sizes.* But if it wasn't a dino, who the fuck was it? She scanned the room, looking for a weapon, but the best she could come up with was a *My Little Pony* umbrella tucked into the back of her closet.

Weapon in hand, and Rainbow Dash ready to do her thing, Victoria cracked the door and peeked out. The house was still fairly dark. A bit of light from the dawning sun entered from the hole in the living room wall and crept down the hall, but whoever had broken into her home hadn't turned on any of the lights.

Why would a burglar turn on the lights? Idiot.

Choking up on the umbrella, Victoria placed her free hand on the spongey material covering the thin metal pole and brought the colorful bludgeon to her shoulder. She tiptoed down the hallway, her left arm rubbing against the wall, and stopped short of the entryway leading to the living room. Something crashed and clattered across the kitchen's linoleum floor.

Her pulse pounded like a snare drum.

"Shit." The voice was hushed--definitely male.

Victoria gasped and shoved her face into the crook of her arm, hoping it had muffled the *yelp* that escaped her lips.

What the fuck, man?

She considered the improvised weapon.

Am I really going to try and beat a man with a Dollar Store *umbrella? That'll end well.*

Shit! The gun.

She glanced at her parents' bedroom and backed down the hall. Her dad kept a loaded 9mm in his closet.

With any luck it's still there.

A shadow encroached on the entryway. Victoria froze. Whoever was in the house was moving in her direction, probably toward the sound she'd made.

Pony Power it is.

When the intruder's head popped around the corner, Victoria swung. Her aim was true. The man shrieked and disappeared back into the living room.

"Shit. What the fuck? Who's here?"

"Your worst fuckin' nightmare, punk!" Victoria was shaking. The umbrella's weight seemed to increase; she struggled to cock it back for another strike. "You better run before I shoot your dumb ass."

"Victoria?"

"Victor?"

Victor peeked around the corner again, rubbing his head. His eyes went wide when they found Victoria standing a few feet away, ready to attack again. "Why the fuck did you hit me?"

Victoria grimaced. "Because I didn't know it was you. Dumbass." She lowered the umbrella to her leg.

Slipping around the corner, Victor eyed Victoria's gaudy weapon. "This is still my house, too, ya know."

"Yeah, so where you been? Mom and dad are gone, their room looks like something out of a horror movie, and there's a giant hole in the living room wall."

"You don't know?" Victor rubbed the back of his neck. "Fuckin' dinosaurs, Vicky. Fuckin'. *Dinosaurs*. They're everywhere. I was at a park with Fiona when one of them burst out of the woods and gobbled her up. Craziest shit I've ever seen. I slept in my car, hoping things would be less clusterfucky in the daylight."

Chastity's final moments—her screams, her body writhing on the bed, the blood—replayed in Victoria's mind. She scowled. "I figured that part out, Braniac. Where the hell did they come from? Is there a real-life Jurassic Park I don't know about?"

Before he could respond Victoria interrupted, slapped him on the shoulder. "And don't call me *Vicky*. You know I hate that shit."

Clutching his arm, Victor said, "Who the fuck knows? Who cares? It's the end of the world out there. I didn't see another living person on my way here. You and me may be the last two people on Earth."

"Jesus Christ."

Maybe Chastity was right. Maybe I am *being punished for kissing girls.*

Frustrated beyond words, Victoria tossed her PDS--Pony Defense System--onto the carpet between them. When it hit the ground, the spring-loaded canopy popped open and leaped into the air. Startled, Victor and Victoria both jumped back as the umbrella floated to the ground.

"Sorry," she said, retrieving the umbrella and tossing it into her room. "What do we do now?"

Victor eyed their parent's bedroom, the blood on the bed and the wall only partially visible from where he stood. "Look for survivors, I guess," he said. "Try not to get eaten."

Rolling her eyes, Victoria shouldered her way past her brother, heading for the kitchen. "Great. We get to live out the plot of every stupid zombie movie, ever. Fan-fucking-tastic."

"Hey, I like zombie movies."

"You would," she said under her breath.

In the kitchen, Victoria made a beeline for the pantry. She threw the door open, grabbed a Ding Dong, ripped the cellophane open--letting it fall to the floor--and shoved the chocolate deliciousness into her mouth. No way the sugar had already hit her bloodstream, but she felt energized after only two bites. Perhaps it was her body's anticipation of sustenance, or something simpler, like mania brought on by the fact that she was still among the living, and not entirely alone anymore.

"Jesus, sis, is that your breakfast?" Victor trudged across the dirty linoleum and opened the fridge.

"What of it?" she mumbled, her mouth still very much full.

"Not exactly healthy."

"If it's the end of the fuckin' world, I'm going to eat what I want, figure be damned. Who do I have to worry about impressing now?"

Victor shrugged. "Good point." He grabbed one of his dad's Boulevard Wheats, pried the cap off with his keychain bottle opener, and chugged the beer.

"Easy there, Hoss." Victoria snatched another Ding Dong and met her brother in front of the refrigerator. "If we're going to survive this shitshow, we'll need to be able to think clearly," she said, and pilfered one of her mom's White Claws.

His bottle now half-empty and near his hip, Victor arched an eyebrow as Victoria popped open the can of hard seltzer and drank deeply.

"Relax." She reached across Victor's chest and pulled the refrigerator door closed, then took another swig of the black-cherry beverage. "You can't get drunk off this crap. It's gluten-free."

"Uh huh." Victor gave her a slow nod, stepped past, then headed for the back door. Outside, he set his bottle down on the round wrought-iron table, dropped into one of the patio chairs, and sighed.

Victoria took the seat across from him and laid her head on top of the seatback. A strange bird circled high above them, disappearing and reappearing behind an ominous storm cloud. It didn't look like any bird Victoria had ever seen, and she wasn't going to spend any time trying to figure out what it was, either.

"Seriously though, Vic, what the hell are we going to do?" she said, still gazing at the odd creature.

"Finding survivors is probably our best bet." He took another swig, started to set the bottle on the table, then brought it back to his leg. "The two of us won't last long against a bunch of dinosaurs."

A lone raindrop splattered square on Victoria's forehead, then ran across her brow and into her hair. A second missed her right eye by only a few millimeters.

That's weird.

"I don't remember it raining during this conversation," she said, lowering her head to look at Vic.

"That's because it didn't."

The clouds dumped all at once and the siblings were caught in a sudden, intense downpour. They were drenched immediately, the rain pounding the rusted table and the warped deck planks.

"I don't understand," she said, hair plastered to her face.

"You need to wake up, Vicky." His voice sounded far away, like he was talking to her from the far side of a tunnel. "Wake up before you drown, sis. Don't let my death be in vain."

§ § §

Victoria's eyes popped open as a mouthful of water slid down her throat. She gagged, coughed, but couldn't raise her head up to expel it. The water lapped up and over her cheeks. The deluge rained down around her, too, raising the water level with impossible speed. She couldn't see her surroundings. What little light managed to crawl down the long tunnel barely penetrated the darkness of the rocky tomb.

The well.

The back of her head throbbed, as did her left arm and upper back. Her butt and legs were buttressed against the wall, jutting straight up; her head rested against another. She'd landed on what remained of the well's roof and that was likely the only reason she hadn't drowned already––a fact that would soon change if she didn't find a way out. She tried maneuvering herself so she could stand, but with her left arm pinned behind her back and her right hand unable to get any purchase on the slick rock wall, it didn't look like she was going anywhere.

"FUCK!" Her voice climbed the well to its mouth, then echoed back.

I'm sorry, Dot.

This was it. She was going to die alone, trapped at the bottom of fucking well, and no one would ever find her. Her last few moments were shaping up to be a *Twilight Zone*-themed episode of *Lassie.*

"What's that, boy? There's a girl trapped in a well? Man, that sucks.

Want to play fetch, then go for a walk, then go to the well and laugh as the girl drinks her last breath?"

Something hit the wall at the top of the well. It bounced off the opposite wall and ricocheted its way down until if finally bounced off Victoria's chest. A second followed a moment later. A rock. Was someone up there?

It took what little strength she had left to yell. "Hello? Anyone there? I'm trapped down here."

A series of pebbles spilled over the lip of the well and pelted her in the face and torso. A moment later a head appeared at the mouth of the tunnel. A head that appeared to be covered in fur.

"Fuck me."

CHAPTER 15

Gotta aim for the head...

Dot awoke to sunshine and a murmuring voice.

"What to do...what to do..."

She sat up and looked around, hunting the voice. Her makeshift chicken-wire cage was still surrounded by the sleeping dinos who'd fucked themselves into comas the night before. They snored like revving motorcycles, the air still redolent of their couplings.

"Oh. Good morning, sweetie," said a voice behind her. Dot twisted on her butt to face it.

The Wicked Bitch had changed clothes and makeup, but it was obvious Dot was in the presence of the same person. Today, they wore a black dress with green fringe around the sleeveless shoulders, with more green about the neck and bottom of the knee-length skirt. And there were those keys again, hanging off their wrist by a neon-green rubber-coil bracelet. A large circular hole was cut in the center of the dress, also outlined in green, that showed off the Bitch's six-pack abs. Their brown skin glistened in the sunlight, as if oiled. Their face was once more done up, but lighter on the pancake foundation this time: ruby-red cheeks, layers of green and gold eyeliner, thick black lashes, and arching eyebrows, as if they were in a perpetual state of shock. If Dot were honest with herself, she thought they looked stunning. Absolutely gorgeous. She'd have killed to have half their talent with makeup.

"Let me out of here," Dot demanded.

"All in due time, pretty. First, I have some questions."

"Fuck you."

"Tsk, tsk, tsk." The Bitch wagged their finger. "I want to know who you're working with. Someone killed one of my friends while I was distracted with you, a lovely Carnotaurus––a failure on my part that I do not wish to repeat. So tell me, who are they?"

"Fuck you," Dot repeated.

The Bitch strode to the cage and grabbed the chicken wire, shoving it inward as far as it would go. Their nails had been done in a green-and-black barber-pole stripes. The design matched their outfit perfectly.

"You owe me, you slag! You murdered my sister, stole her familiar, and I can only *imagine* decided to ride on my community with the aid of that friend. Tell me. Who. You. Are. Working with!"

Dot got to her feet and approached the Bitch where they stood on the other side of the chicken wire. Dot smiled coyly as she reached for their hand, maintaining eye contact with them. In a quick motion, she grabbed the middle finger of their left hand and bent it backward against the wire. The Bitch shrieked and snatched their hands away. They clutched their injured hand to their chest.

"Bitch!" they shrieked.

"You're one to talk."

"Stanley!" the Bitch roared. "Stanley, here! To me!"

A great pounding sounded. The earth quaked. Dot grabbed hold of the chicken wire to maintain her balance as she watched the trees in the distance shake and sway. From between the trunks came a T-Rex almost twice the size of Sue. The lumbering beast roared as it broke from the tree line. Dot could smell its breath from fifty yards: carrion and rot. Motherfucker needed to brush his teeth.

Hey, where is Sue? Dot thought, before her mind switched back to more pressing issues.

The Rex stomped through the slumbering dinos, and Dot thought it looked as if it were being a bit careful, so as not to step on any of its brethren. Onward it came, all screeching roars and gnashing teeth. Stanley reached Dot's cage, bent down, and tore the chicken-wire prison away with his mouth. Dot fell backward and landed hard on her tailbone. Her teeth clicked, sending bolts of agony into her brain. The Rex slung the cage into the distance, where it broke apart on top of a sleeping triceratops that didn't so much as flinch, leaving Dot completely vulnerable. He leaned down, opened his maw, and roared in her face, splattering her with spittle and chunks of what could only be old, rotten meat. Dot struggled to keep her gorge down, and somehow succeeded.

"Down, boy," said the Bitch. "Not yet. Not just yet."

Stanley rose to his full height and took a step back. Dot, heart beating a "Wipeout" rhythm in her chest, stayed on her ass.

The Bitch said, "You will tell me why you came here, or Stanley will bite you in half and leave your legs so he'll have a snack for later. Tell. Me."

"Fuck. You."

Dot could see the hesitancy in their eyes. The Bitch didn't dare approach. Dot had already proven she had no qualms about hurting them, yet they moved forward, closing the distance, before stopping a foot out of reach.

"You and your people, whoever they are, have been trying to take this land from us for as long as I can recall. I warded off their advances because my army is far greater than theirs, but I have lost as much as them, if not more. With my sister dead, I am all alone, and still they come for me. If you will not tell me who they are, you will die, my pretty, and your little dinosaur, too."

Dot glanced over her shoulder to where Tutu stood in his cage, silent yet vigilant. She'd forgotten about him, distracted as she was.

"It's okay, boy. Nothing's gonna happen to you," she reassured the raptor before facing the Bitch once again. "I'm not working with anyone. I'm here on my own. To stop you."

"Why don't I believe that?"

Dot shrugged. "I don't give a flying fuck what you believe. You killed most of the world with your fuckin' spell, and I'm here to return the favor."

"Spell?" The Bitch looked honestly confused. "What spell?"

"Oh, fuck you," Dot said with a mirthless laugh. "I was told what you and your sister did. Buncha *The Craft* rejects, fuckin' with magic and shit. My aunt and uncle are dead because of you, so save me your outrage and fake-ass surprise. You did this. You and your cunt sister."

The Bitch squinted at Dot. "Who told you that?"

"Does it matter?"

"Yes, it does, because it's all lies. We didn't cause this. We have—*had*—been trying to reverse it. In fact, that's what Belinda was trying to do before you murdered her. She'd travelled to the source of the outbreak as a last-ditch effort, into the land of our enemy, attempting to save us. Now that you've killed my sister, I am left to shoulder the burden alone."

"If you think I'm going to believe a word you say, you're dumber than a box of hammers and half as sharp."

"The people to the north. They're the ones who sent you." These were not questions.

"Fuck you."

The Bitch glared. "Honey, they don't want revenge for what they told you we did. They want our water."

"Liar."

"Oh? Is that so? Tell me, how do you think I maintain this fabulous look of mine? You're a fine-looking girl without any makeup, but to think you've never worn and had to remove any of your own is more unbelievable to me than my story is to you. It takes water to stay this fresh looking. It's the only way to slay, my pretty."

"They have water," Dot lied. But it was only a small lie, because Leo's crew did have water, albeit in short and ever-dwindling supply. The condensation rig on the roof wasn't anything that could be relied on, but it had kept them alive this long.

"Then they're just opposed to showers. Seems legit." The sarcasm dripped from the Bitch's words.

"Okay, RuPaul, how the fuck do you have running water here at the end of the world?"

"Why should I answer your questions when you won't answer mine?"

"I don't really care one way or another. You're gonna lie either way. Just wanted to see how far you'd go with your—"

"There's an underground stream that runs all through this property and beyond. Well water, local folks called it. Even some of the houses in the nearby suburb the apes have claimed ran off this source before the world moved on. Hell, some of them even had working wells, like they were a bunch of Podunk cowboys or something. Believe me or not, my pretty, but it's true. They're not mad because they think my sister and I killed the world. They're greedy, the bunch of colonizers. I would have helped them, but they attacked me first. They kill my friends and call it self-defense. They want to steal *our* land and call *us* the villains. But, alas, that is the American way, is it not?"

"If you know who they are, why do you keep asking me who I'm with?"

"Because I had hopes that you were truly on your own. I had hopes of finding a...Never mind. It doesn't matter. You've all but said you're working with them, so there's no reason to keep you alive any longer. Stanley, eat the bitch, but save the shoes. Thank you."

Stanley charged. Dot rolled. The Rex slammed his face into the grass where she'd been only a second before. She lurch-crawled to her feet and ran, pushing past and through the pain of her sprained ankle. The Rex's thunderous footsteps closed the distance in only a few steps. Dot juked left but went right. The Rex stumbled, almost went down, but kept coming. Dot wove through the sleeping dinosaurs, thinking, even in her terror, that it was so fucking odd none of them had awoken during all this. They must be under the Bitch's control. That was the only logical explanation...

Then a thought occurred to her.

The shoes. She'd forgotten about her goddamn shoes.

"WAKE UP!" she screamed, her voice carrying far and wide.

The slumbering dinosaurs came alive, all at the same time: triceratops stretched like awakening dogs, forepaws forward, asses in the air; long-necks at the perimeter of the herd rose, heads scraping the heavens; raptors zipped and zoomed this way and that, as energetic as sugar-fueled toddlers. The world rumbled with the sounds of moving dinosaurs.

"HELP ME!" Dot cried as the Rex once more closed the distance.

In her peripheral vision, she saw a triceratops charging. She tracked its movement by craning her neck, and just barely saw it collide, horns first, into one of the Rex's scaly thighs. The Rex shrieked, lost its balance, and crashed onto his side. Dot came to a sliding halt in the grass. Everything in her fought to keep moving, knew she had to escape, but a stronger part of her wanted to see this, wanted to see the Rex felled and stopped for good.

This, however, would not be the outcome.

On its side, the Rex snapped its massive jaws in the direction of the impact-stunned triceratops and bit its entire face off in one mighty chomp. Blood spewed from the stump of the creature's head. The half of its brain that remained in its skull slipped from the cavity and plopped onto the grass.

"Fuck," Dot said breathlessly.

The faceless triceratops stumbled to one side, then the other, before falling over, its dying legs kicking as if it were once again charging. Dot felt more than a modicum of sorrow for the poor thing. It was dead because she had called it to help her. She'd sacrificed a life to save her own.

"No!" the Bitch screamed. "Don't hurt family!"

Family...

"Sue!" Dot hollered. "Sue, come!"

In the distance, a roar, then a pounding of massive feet. Sue broke through the trees close to where Stanley had emerged, shaking her head, as if trying to shoo away a nasty nightmare. Sue's eyes met Dot's, and she came running.

"Stanley!" Dot yelled. "Get Stanley!"

Sue charged.

"No!" the Bitch roared. "Stop!"

Sue skidded to a halt.

"Shit," Dot groaned.

This wasn't going to be as easy as she'd first expected it would be.

"Call him off!" Dot yelled over the sizable distance between her and the Bitch.

"Truce, goddamn it, truce!" the Bitch replied.

"Truce!" Dot hollered back.

Stanley got to his feet with a concerted effort but did not attack. He stood between Dot and the Bitch, awaiting instructions.

"There's no need for—" the Bitch started but their words were cut off by a single sound: a loud and echoing *POP!*

The Bitch pirouetted and dropped like a pile of bricks thrown from a rooftop. Stanley fell simultaneously, crashing down onto his side, his eyes closing. Dot thought for a moment that he'd died, that whatever had fallen his master had killed him as well, but no; the Rex's flanks rose and fell with breath. He was only unconscious.

Dot dashed around the fallen Rex and across the field, weaving through meandering dinosaurs that shuffled to and fro like bored children, and stopped a few feet from where the Bitch had crumpled. Blood drained from underneath their head to pool in the grass. Not a lot, but enough to be noticeable.

"Finally got the bitch!" Crow cried as he limped from the trees opposite from where Stanley and Sue had joined the party. He had an arm around Leo's neck, and both men were grinning like fools. Foil in his power armor came next. Victor and, more importantly, Victoria were nowhere in sight.

Dot heard movement and glanced back to where the Bitch had fallen. They had rolled over and were glaring at Dot with wide, menacing eyes. A wicked looking gash ran from the corner of one eye, across their temple, and around to a gory mess that Dot assumed had once been an ear. The Bitch was injured but far from dead.

And, holy shit, did they look pissed.

"Kill them," the Bitch hissed. "Kill them all."

Every dinosaur in attendance heeded their master's call.

CHAPTER 16

A test of wills

The ragtag group of humans shuffled toward the center of the clearing, while a handful more dinos of varying size and species emerged from the woods behind them. Standing upright, Stanley raised his head and roared into the air. Sue responded and stepped around the band of misfits, heading toward the great beast.

"We're in the shit, now," Crow said, hobbling up to Dot, still using Leo to help support his weight. The sniper's other arm hung lifelessly at his side, and Dot wondered if he'd been injured in a previous battle. She also wanted to know how he'd fired his rifle, hurt like he was.

Dot eyed the T-Rexes as they squared off, worried that Sue wouldn't last long against her much larger male opponent. But what could she do? Sue may not have been responding to the Bitch's indirect order to attack, but she had complied to their command to stop. The Bitch could apparently control all the beasts.

Shit. That's it! I'm such an idiot.

"EVERYONE STOP!" Dot's voice echoed across the glade, halting the dinos and humans in their tracks. Spinning back toward the Bitch, she said, "You can't win this, and you know it. You need to back off, now, before we wipe out what little of humanity is left!"

"Yeah, back off, bitch, so I can put you down for good." Leo reached into his waistband and pulled out his sidearm, although he did not aim the gun. It hung near his leg, the barrel tapping anxiously against his thigh.

"Sue?" Dot said, without taking her eyes away from the Bitch.

Sue turned, lowered her head to within a few feet of Leo and Crow, and roared. The pair stumbled back, as much from fear as the force of Sue's bellowing breath, and fell on their asses. Crow screamed in pain when he landed. Leo looked nonplussed.

"What the fuck, Dot?" Leo hollered.

"Yeah, the fuck?" Crow echoed in a high, whiny voice that belied the man's macho veneer.

"No one else is dying," Dot said, glancing at the knuckleheads scrambling back to their feet. "The five of us are going to have a conversation, like adults. And if anyone gets uppity, Sue is going to eat them."

Sue grunted. It almost sounded like a laugh. Perhaps the smaller Rex was simply excited at the prospect of a future meal.

"And speaking of the five of us," Dot continued, "where are the twins?"

Leo and Crow side-eyed each other, mumbling, but not really saying anything. Foil powered down his armor and hopped out, moving toward the group.

"They're gone," he said. He stopped near the other two men and frowned. "Victor saw you fall into the trees and we came looking for you. When we arrived at the neighborhood where the apes had been camped, we were attacked by a horned Rex. We lost contact with Victor and Victoria in the fray. I'm sorry."

Dot's stomach dropped. She was going to puke. She took three deep breaths to ward off the nausea.

"They're...they're dead?" she stammered.

"That's what we're assuming. I'm so sorry, Dot." And Foil did look sorry. She wasn't sure why the emotion in his eyes surprised her. She supposed she'd figured him for a heartless hardass, but that didn't seem to be the case. Yet, she couldn't help but notice the verbiage he'd used. Had they not looked for the twins? Had they simply left them behind to move on with their mission? Weren't these guys American soldiers? Whatever happened to no man (or woman) left behind?

Dot's blood ignited. Her face twisted into a scowl. "*Assuming*? You don't know? You left them behind without confirming whether they were alive or dead?"

"There was no sign of them. We searched for hours. Nothing." Foil's eyes flitted in every direction but Dot's. He was lying, and she knew it.

"If that horny bastard got them," Crow said, "there wouldn't've been much left."

Seizing the opportunity, the Bitch hopped to their feet and yelled, "Stanley, sweep the leg!"

With a speed none of them could have expected, Stanley lowered to his haunches and whipped his tail around, slamming it into one of Sue's legs. The giant beast bellowed as she fell on her flank, pinning Crow, Leo, and Foil beneath her.

"What were you saying about me not being able to win?" The Bitch gave Dot a wide, toothy grin, a gleeful glint in their eye that turned eerie once Dot took in the blood running down the Bitch's face from the wound scratched from eye to temple.

Fuck me.

Dot spun and took off running. She sprinted past her helpless comrades as they struggled to free themselves; her thundering pulse and the Bitch's footfalls drawing closer filled her ears. She zigzagged around another dinosaur standing in place--waiting for another command from one of its masters--

and reached Foil's power armor with seconds to spare. She jumped in, sealed the hatch, and scoured the control panel, desperate to find the power button.

The Bitch slammed into the mech, pounding on the canopy with their fists. "Come out, come out, my pretty. Fight me like the bitch I know you are."

"I'm not really one for a fair fight," Dot said, locating the ignition and powering up the mech. The metal monster whirred to life, the pistons raising it up to full height. The Bitch jumped back, but not before Dot grabbed hold of a joystick on the center console and swung Newt around, smacking the Bitch in the chest with its gigantic right arm.

The Bitch howled. The impact sent them tumbling backward, head over ass. Stanley roared in the distance, lumbering toward Dot.

"This should be fun," Dot said under her breath.

Familiarizing herself with the machine's controls, she gripped the independent joysticks and slung Newt's arms back and forth, left and right, getting a feel for their range and speed. A pair of clamps had secured her feet in the stirrups when the power came on. The snug fit allowed her to make natural walking movements to power the pistons in the legs.

Now, if this thing had a canon or a god damned rocket launcher, we'd really be in business.

The bitch had rolled halfway to where the three men were still pinned under Sue. Stanley had passed the lot of them, closing on Dot: mouth open wide, teeth bared. Realizing that there were two likely avenues of attack, Dot needed to determine what strategy the giant creature would use so she could react. Once it was in range, it could pull its head back and snap it at her like a snake, transferring a good amount of kinetic force but remaining out of Newt's range. Or it could simply trample her.

She was only going to get one shot at this. If either attack landed, she'd be knocked off balance. She'd seen Stanley use that fancy leg sweep, but that was at the command of the Bitch. This time, though, they hadn't issued a directive; Stanley was running on instinct, protecting his master, which meant he would probably try to trample Dot. Given his size and strength advantage, it was the route she herself would use, were their roles reversed.

As soon as the lizard was in range, she swung Newt's left arm at his head. To both her and Stanley's surprise, her strike connected. The armored clamp smashed into the beast's jaw, sending him reeling. Before the Bitch's pet could react, Dot spun Newt's right clamp, opened it, and used it to grab Stanley by the throat.

The giant creature tried pulling away, using his legs to free himself from Newt's grasp. Dot had to take the right stick in both hands to keep from being overpowered. Every internal sensor and siren began to sound. Stanley was taxing Newt's power and strength, redlining every visible gauge. But if Dot lost her grip, she was dead. It wouldn't take long for the monster to chew through Newt's armor and pluck her from inside. She wondered what it would feel like to be eaten alive. Would she die quickly, or would she know the sensation of being swallowed and digested before she finally ran out of air?

"Dot! What the hell are you doing?" Leo had freed his leg from under Sue and was inching away.

"WHAT DOES IT LOOK LIKE?"

"Use the damn shoes. Tell it to stand down."

Except she couldn't, not while she was focused on piloting Newt. Dot didn't fully understand how the slippers worked, but she knew it took more than words to control the dinos. It took an ass-load of concentration, and she didn't have the mental fortitude to carry out both tasks at the same time. Then again, if she didn't at least try, she was going to die bloody and screaming.

"STOP!" Something in Dot's neck popped. She'd pulled something straining to yell while using all her strength to keep the dino in Newt's grip. "Stanley..." she said through gritted teeth. "sit."

Stanley did just the opposite. He reared back, causing sparks to pop off Newt's right arm in all directions. The super-heated particles rained down on the forest floor like a sparkler on the 4th of July. That was when Dot realized her left foot was cold. The metal stirrup and clamp were pressed against her bare skin.

She'd lost one of the shoes.

No wonder Stanley wasn't listening.

Shit...

Goosebumps shot up her legs and crawled down her arms. Her stomach leaped into her chest. It was suddenly hard to breathe.

"Awe, does the siren's song no longer affect my pet monster?" The Bitch was back on their feet, grinning like an idiot and looking like the gaudiest Bond villain, ever. They were, however, injured. One of their arms was crossed over their chest where the power armor's arm had struck them. If the Bitch survived this day, they were going to have one hell of a bruise. "That's a shame. I guess you won't have the power to stop him from eviscerating you, now. And since you won't be around to see it, you should know your friends will--"

Newt's left arm crashed into Stanley's jaw, dazing the creature, and relieving the pressure on the right arm.

"Call him off, Bitch." Dot swung the mech's free arm around again, connecting with the T-Rex square in the jaw and dislodging teeth. "Call him off!"

But the Bitch didn't move, didn't speak. They just stood there, slack jawed, eyes wide, swaying back and forth like they were going to pass out.

Dot was about to strike Stanley again, but something behind the mountainous carnivore caught her attention.

Sue.

She was on her feet again, moving towards Stanley and Dot, but was she on her way to help, or to join the attack against Dot?

Rubbing her big toe against the felt lining of her left shoe, Dot prayed the contact would be enough. "Sue," she cried. "Kill the Bitch."

Sue stopped in her oversized tracks, did an about face, and stomped across the clearing, bearing down on her former master's sibling.

"No!" The Bitch dropped to their knees, hands in the air. "Stop. Everyone stand down. Just don't hurt him anymore."

Sue stopped her charge, and Stanley went limp in Newt's grip. All the other dinos in the surrounding area lay down.

Dot closed her eyes and sighed.

"Truce," the Bitch said. "I mean it this time. Let's talk this shit out."

"Fuck that!" the familiar voice exploded from the forest as more than a dozen apes burst through the tree line, forming a perimeter around the clearing. "This ends now!"

And there she was, riding a gorilla the size of a 'roided-out grizzly bear like the god damned queen of the jungle. A beautiful and welcome sight.

Victoria.

CHAPTER 17

The Chase is On...

Multiple things happened all at once:

The apes attacked, leaping this way and that, attaching themselves to dinosaurs of varying shapes and sizes. One ape was instantly torn to shreds by a velociraptor twice the size of Tutu. The two-legged bird-like creature feasted on the ape's guts until another ape swung in with a rock and bashed the birdie's head in.

While that was going down, the Bitch had gotten to their feet and was screaming orders to their army of giant lizards, flailing their arms about as if they were an orchestra conductor sped up to times-three speed.

And while the Bitch was busy, Dot was working on getting Newt moving again, because Stanley was headed for Tutu's cage with a hungry, sinister gleam in his eyes. Half of Newt's controls didn't work, but Dot found that if she jammed the right joystick in any given direction, the armor's right arm tracked her movement. She used the pinchers to dig into the dirt and drag the power armor forward, foot by foot, but she wasn't going to make it in time. Stanley dipped low and clamped down on Tutu's chicken-wire cage with his powerful jaws. He flung the cage away.

"No!" Dot screamed as the shooting began.

Crow had his long-gun up and was blasting the shit out of anything that moved, which was everything. He shot from the hip, the stock of the rifle jammed into his armpit, because his other arm was useless. He blew the head off a charging raptor, then shot a triceratops between the eyes as it rushed Leo. The massive, three-horned creature's front legs folded, and the beast carved a trench into the ground as it slid forward on its chest, its horns stopping a mere half a foot from Leo.

"Thanks," Leo told Crow.

"Don't mention it," Crow responded, and then returned to firing at anything with a goddamn pulse.

Foil lasted all of thirty-nine seconds without his power armor. Sue, now outside of Dot's control, snatched the man up and ground him to paste in her mouth. He died screaming.

Back to Dot. Seconds before Stanley was able to make a snack out of her little friend Tutu, Dot swung the arm of the power armor around and latched onto Stanley's tail. Her thumb dug into the pressure sensitive button that worked the clamp, smashing the Rex's tail to pulp. The Rex roared and twisted from side to side, trying to rip his tail from the grip of the power armor. Dot held her thumb flush with the button, refusing to let go, and said, "Not so fuckin' wicked now, are you, you fuckin' fuckface fuck!"

Stanley screeched, whipped around, and his tail came off. Dot had time to say "Oh," before Stanley caromed into her. The power armor went down hard, jarring every bone in Dot's body as it slammed into the grass. Dirt and sod exploded when the armor hit, as if a bomb had gone off. Dot's foot came out of her remaining shoe, and she was tossed about the cab like a crash test dummy.

While Dot was busy trying not to get eaten, Leo was focused on the Bitch. He raised his sidearm, aimed, and was flung to the side as something crashed into Crow, who then crashed into him. They went down like a row of dominos. Leo cussed as he fell, and Crow landed on top of him. Crow's AR-15 spat fire as the man screamed and thrashed on top of Leo. Blood seemed to spill from every inch of Crow as he was mauled by an unseen…*something*.

Victoria rode the giant gorilla into battle, brandishing a hatchet in one hand as she went. Why they were helping her was as much of a mystery as their eagerness to join the fray, but Victoria wasn't inclined to look a gift horse in the mouth by inquiring as to their motivations. Besides, she didn't speak ape, so how the fuck was she gonna ask in the first place?

Dot scrambled around inside the cab of the grounded power armor, drawing her knees to her chest to make sure her bare feet didn't peek from the cab for Stanley to munch on. The Rex's jaws clamped down on the suit, hefted it into the air, and sent Dot and all flying. She crashed down some twenty feet away and ricocheted off Newt's interior like a manic pinball. Everything hurt, all at once. Tears sprung from her eyes, but even through her blurred vision, she could see Tutu slinking forward.

He didn't look happy to see her. He looked mad. Truth be told, he looked fucking *hungry*.

"No, boy. Back, boy. Good Tutu. Fuck shit fuck shit *fuckin' shit*!"

Tutu was small enough to slide effortlessly into the cab, and Dot could see his intentions, so she rushed out of one side, just as he was entering the other. The fact she'd now shed both of her shoes in the melee was not lost on her. The realization hit her brain and adrenaline burst into her bloodstream. She was unarmed and barefoot, without aid of weapon or magic shoes, and the dinosaur she'd befriended, who she assumed hadn't eaten in over twenty-four hours, was currently scrabbling from the power armor where she'd left him.

This.

Was not.

Good.

She dashed around dinosaurs, juking left and right, shoulder-checking the leg of a brontosaurus. The impact jarred her, but somehow she stayed on her feet. She spun away and leaned into a run, pain slicing through her bare feet as they came down on all kinds of rocks and sticker burs and who knew what else. Her sprained ankle was a ball of molten lava but adrenaline was a kind mistress. Into the trees she ran, and Tutu followed, all flashing claws and snapping teeth.

Dot used to laugh at scared teenage girls as they fled into the woods, away from one masked killer or another. But this wasn't a horror movie. This was real life, or at least whatever constituted real life now. She wasn't playing hide and go fuck yourself with Jason Vorhees. She was fleeing the possibility of becoming future dinosaur shit. Running in a straight line through a forest was an impossibility due to the sporadic placement of the trees. She could only zig and zag through them. Furthermore, if she maintained a clean direction from Point A to Point B, wherever the fuck Point B should be, Tutu would be on her in an instant. No way she could outrun the little fucker. So she cut in front of trees, dashed left, rushed right, zigzagging through unknown territory until her lungs were aflame and her circulatory system pumped lava.

She knew she wouldn't be able to keep this up for long. She was going to die; she knew it. It was an eventuality. But she was no quitter. She would run until her body gave up, and then she would fall. Hopefully, she could get back up and fight, but the possibility of that happening was dwindling by the second.

She threw out an arm; clotheslined a tree trunk, the bark digging into her skin, which hurt like a motherfucker; and slung herself around, doing a complete one-eighty. She heard Tutu skid past as she took off again, back in the direction of the battle waging in the field. She could hear him correct course, tracking her once more. She doubted she would make it back to the fight, but she had to try.

Had to...

Keep...

Going.

Up ahead, an oddity. Something big and black and the size of a bus's grille was barreling toward her. From the thing's back, Victoria shouted, "Duck!"

Dot did more than duck. She dove between the gorilla's legs. It sailed over her as she rolled to watch what happened next.

Tutu leaped.

The gorilla reared back. Tutu soared forward, his jaws wide, and the gorilla cold-clocked the bird-like dinosaur, sending Tutu slamming into the trunk of a great oak. Victoria hopped off the gorilla and ran to Dot. She helped Dot to her feet and swallowed her in a tight embrace. Next thing either one of them knew, they were kissing. It was wonderful and beautiful and wholly inappropriate, given the urgency of their situation.

Dot pushed away: not because she wanted to, but because she had to. She was not going to die kissing this woman, no matter how fucking hot for Victoria she was at that moment. Victoria frowned with disappointment, but Dot could tell she understood. They had bigger fish to fry, and they were gonna need a bigger goddamn boat.

"Bobo," Victoria called, and the gorilla approached.

"Bobo?" Dot said with a small laugh. "You two old friends, or some shit?"

"No. I can't even talk to them, but he seems to respond to that name. Comes from a show I saw when I was a kid, *Bobo and Marcy's Idiot Hour.* It probably wasn't the best show for kids, but—"

"Victoria, baby, you're rambling."

"Right, sorry. By the way," Victoria said as she took something from Bobo the Gorilla's meaty fist. "You look better in these than I do."

Dot screamed when she saw the lizard-skin shoes Victoria was holding. She wrapped her arms around her and squeezed until Victoria's feet left the ground.

"You're my fuckin' hero," she said, probably a little too loudly into Victoria's ear.

"You're damn straight, I am. I've always wanted to save a princess from a castle like a Mario brother." Victoria was grinning so hard when Dot pulled away that Dot almost cried with relief. She had thought she'd never see that smile again.

"Shall we?" Victoria said, pointing back toward the battle.

"We shall. Time to end this fuckin' thing."

Dot slipped the shoes on her feet and turned around, ready and willing to fuck shit up.

CHAPTER 18:

So Long, and Thanks for all the Dinos

Running next to Victoria, who was still riding Bobo and giving off a sexy cowgirl vibe that Dot hadn't realized she'd found attractive until that moment, Dot nodded, and the two of them veered diagonally, in opposite directions, toward the battle. Victoria and Bobo pulled ahead with just a few quick strides. Dot's calves burned, her breath coming hard and fast. The small break, between running away from Tutu and racing back to the battlefield, hadn't been long enough for her body to recuperate. Victoria would re-enter the fray well ahead of her, and Dot still had no idea how she was going to wrestle control of the dinos away from the Bitch.

A triceratops lying a few feet from the tree line noticed Dot as she approached. Probably the mate of the one Crow had bullseyed between the eyes before he was ripped apart.

"Here, girl," Dot called, pouring on as much speed as her tired body could muster.

The horned beast lumbered to her legs, snorted, then trotted toward Dot. When she stopped a few feet away from Dot, Dot leapt, grabbed the plate at the base of the triceratops' skull, and swung herself around and onto the creature's back. Then, kicking her heels into the sides of her new stead's chest, she yelled, "YAH!"

Pointy––as Dot had decided to call the triceratops––was much faster than Dot had supposed. She held Pointy's skull plate with both hands as they darted around trees and over some woodland animals. They burst into the clearing at a full gallop and were greeted by unintelligible shouting and gunfire.

Leo had ducked behind Stanley's severed tail and was taking pot shots at the Bitch, who was hiding behind the bronto that had almost smashed Dot into roadkill. Victoria and Bobo were circling behind their fearless leader, engaging a swarm of raptors that poured into the glade form the north. Bobo trampled two or three before one slipped past, only to have its head severed from its body by Victoria's hatchet.

Where the hell did she find a hatchet?

Off near the felled power armor, Stanley was licking his wounds and ducking a shrewdness of apes swinging out of the trees, lunging at him, feetfirst. Sue, on the other hand, had engaged the furry proto-humans, slamming her tail into the hapless creatures on the ground and plucking others from the trees with her teeth, chomping them into gooey paste.

Dot steered Pointy towards the bronto's leg––and the Bitch behind it––and kicked her heels once more into her stead's flanks. Pointy punched it to warp speed, all four feet off the ground more than they touched it, as the pair zipped toward the mountainous herbivore. Less than twenty feet away, Dot glanced over her shoulder and shouted, "SUE! Kill Stanley!"

"What? No!" The Bitch's head popped out from behind the leg. They were about to issue their own command when Pointy rammed into the brontosaurus. The Bitch careened backwards from the impact, just before the giant beast plummeted to the ground. A shot sounded as the Bitch rolled away from the falling dinosaur. They cried out as blood spat from their arm.

The glancing bullet then drilled into the bronto's leg. The creature bellowed; its roar trailing its long neck as it crashed into the trees, toppling them, one and all.

When the two lizards collided, Dot was catapulted over Pointy's head. She bounced off the brontosaurus's leg a second before it fell, hit the ground, then rolled backward. Pointy kept on the same path she'd been traveling. The horned widow sauntered into the forest and disappeared.

While Dot and Pointy were busy flushing out the Bitch, Sue had discarded her shit-flinging chew toys and was bearing down on Stanley. Lying on his side, the maimed Rex never had a chance. He raised his head as Sue closed on him, then howled. The Queen of the Dinos tore a manhole-sized chunk out of his neck. Blood splattered across Sue's face. His head fell to the ground, and Sue went in for another bite. Just to be sure.

"NO!" The Bitch pushed off the ground, eyes big and watery. "You filthy slut. You KILLED him! You killed my *baby*!" They glanced from their dead pet to Dot, then to Leo. With the big guy out of commission, Leo was resting lazily across Stanley's tail, both hands wrapped around the pistol's grip, sighting the Bitch.

"Got you now, bitch." Leo's body tensed. He pulled the trigger. But not before one of the raptor reinforcements managed to slip by Victoria and slashed the man across the back of his leg with its hooked foot talon. "Gah! Sonofabitch!" The shot went wide. Leo fell to his knees, the gun dropping to the ground next to him.

The Bitch was on the move, gnashing their teeth, sprinting toward Leo. Victoria saw it too. She brought Bobo around and charged, but as fast as the giant gorilla was, they wouldn't make it to Leo before the Bitch did.

Time to be a hero.

Dot blew out a breath, lowered her head, and dug into a run. Heartbeat thundering like Sue's foot falls, she knew she wasn't going to be beat the Bitch to Leo. Pumping her arms and legs harder and faster, her breathing like that of a pregnant woman who'd been denied an epidural, Dot realized she didn't need to beat them there. She only needed to get past the Bitch before they shot her.

The Bitch hopped over Stanley's tail, one hand on his scales propelling them over, swinging both legs around. They kicked Leo hard in the chest with both feet and fell on their ass, drop-kick-style. Scrambling to their hands and knees, the Bitch went for Leo's pistol.

There was no way on God's green Earth that Dot could overpower the drag queen, even injured. Their biceps were nearly the size of Dot's head, and they were running on pure, balls-to-the-wall anger and adrenaline. So, instead of slamming into them, she dove over, tucked into a ball, and rolled combat-style past Leo and right into Crow's body.

"Dot, move!"

Leo's voice told Dot what she already knew: the Bitch had his gun. She leaped over Crow as the shot rang out. The bullet grazed her thigh before burrowing into Crow's left eye and blasting out the back of his skull. Dot landed flat on her stomach. The impact stole her breath.

A second report sounded as Dot rolled onto her back, the ground around her geysering grass and dirt. She raised her eyes to meet the Bitch's gaze and smiled. Dot had Crow's long-gun in hand, the barrel zeroed in on the Bitch's junk.

"Willing to risk it?" Dot said. "You can live without that ear, but I'm willing to bet you won't want to live without your shit." She nodded at the Bitch's crotch, her finger resting on the trigger.

Victoria and Bobo arrived on Dot's left, but too far away to intervene. The Bitch gave them the side-eye before addressing Dot. "Tell Tarzana to back off. I've got more than enough bullets for all of you."

Bobo snorted.

Victoria raised the hatchet to her shoulder.

"Babe, no. I've got this." Dot didn't dare take her eyes off the Bitch.

"We're going to talk this out and find a bloodless resolution."

Leo dragged himself out from underneath the Bitch, moving toward the space between Dot and Victoria. "You can't trust that bitch, Dot. Just pull the trigger."

"Said the conniving lion," the Bitch said, glancing at Leo. "If it weren't for you, we wouldn't be in this mess, now would we?"

"I don't know what you're talking about. It was you and your sister who attacked us."

The Bitch laughed. "You should consider a career in editing. Your revision skills are staggering."

Dot shifted her gaze to the ground behind and adjacent to the Bitch. Leo's diversion had given her the time she needed to test her theory about the scaled shoes' control over the dinos being telepathic, rather than verbal.

"What are you looking at, whore?" The Bitch twisted at the neck.

Dot would've liked to think the last thing that went through their head was: *Fuck me, that bitch has skills*. But she'd never know.

Tutu leaped from behind the Bitch, sailing past them, and taking a softball-size chunk out of their throat with his claws.

Grabbing their own neck with both hands, the Bitch flung their head back toward Dot, eyes bulging, blood pouring from between their fingers and running down their chest. Their mouth moved as if they were trying to speak, but blood was the only thing that managed to spill out.

Raising the long-gun's barrel, Dot said, "And a murder of raptors sing thee to thy rest."

She pulled the trigger. The blast kicked the rifle back harder than Dot expected. It slammed into the crook of her arm, then flipped up and over her shoulder. The bullet obliterated the Bitch's teeth, propelling enamel shards in every direction, like shrapnel off a frag grenade. Then it blew out the back of their skull.

The Bitch crumpled to the ground.

"Ding-dong, the bitch is——"

"Don't, Leo." Cringing, Dot struggled to her feet, the graze-wound burning when she put weight on her right leg. "Just, don't."

Victoria jumped from Bobo's back and hit the ground running. She raced to Dot's side. Dot listed to the right, threatening to collapse, but Victoria caught her before she went down.

"I got you," Victoria said. All around them, the remaining dinos laid down and closed their eyes. Sue curled up next to Stanley's corpse and drifted into dreamland.

Back on his feet, Leo eyed the two of them, giving Victoria a thin smile. "What happened to you, girl? We looked all around that neighborhood."

"Did you look in the well, behind the house I ran into?"

"The well?" Dot and Leo said in a fucked-up harmony, melding surprise, confusion, and disbelief.

Dot and Victoria hobbled to Stanley's severed tail——the middle section, which only rose a few feet from the ground——so Dot could get off her injured leg.

"The damn Carnotaraus knocked me in after it ate Victor," Victoria said.

"Oh, sweetie, I'm so sorry." Dot grimaced then kissed Victoria on the cheek.

The other girl forced a smile.

"How did you get out?" Leo collected his gun before moving to the Bitch's side to check their pulse——which seemed all together strange, given that more than half their head was a smoldering crater. Like Dot, he was favoring his uninjured leg. The slash wound from the raptor would need stitches before it would heal.

Victoria nodded at Bobo. "These guys. A bunch of the smaller ones chain-ganged themselves down the well and hauled my sorry ass up."

Dot snorted a little laugh. "Hey, I like your ass."

Victoria chuckled, patting Dot on the thigh. "That escalated quickly."

"Jesus Christ. Get a room," Leo said. He scooted to the Bitch's feet, and not so gingerly, pried their shoes off. It looked like they'd fit him, if not a little snuggly. Surprisingly, he didn't slip them on and tucked them instead, under his arm.

"What about the tomahawk?" Dot motioned for Tutu. The turkeysaurus hopped to his feet and waddled over. "Find that in the well, did ya?"

"No, dork. It was in a garage. I grabbed it before the apes and I headed out to save your ass."

"That makes more sense," Dot said, and leaned forward to pet Tutu on his feathered head.

Reaching for Crow's gun, Leo said, "You chicks ready to motor?"

Dot glanced across the battlefield, noting the bodies: Stanley, the Bitch, Crow, Foil. So much death, but she was oddly numb to it all. She'd not known these men well enough to mourn them, even if she thought that any life lost was a tragedy.

"Yeah," she said. "Let's get the fuck out of here."

CHAPTER 19

There's No Place Like Home...

But instead of heading North, Leo headed West, toward the tree line, and farther away from *Homosapien Park*. He had Crow's long-gun slung over one shoulder, and he was whistling, happier than a pig in shit. If the wound in his leg was causing him any pain, Dot couldn't tell from the way he was acting.

It was as she watched him walking away that Dot noticed the keys on his right wrist. They were the same keys the Bitch had had on her own wrist. What they were for, Dot didn't know, but she planned to find out.

"Hey!" she called after him. "Where are you going?"

"Tag along and find out, why don't'cha?"

She'd never heard him so jovial. Of course, she barely knew they guy, but she'd not taken him for anyone capable of being chipper.

"What's got into him?" Victoria asked, confirming Dot's assumption that Leo simply didn't act this way.

The two women glanced at one another and back to Leo as he strode away. They had no other choice but to follow.

By the time they'd caught up with him, Dot recognized where they were—the exact place Stanley had come crashing through the trees when he made his initial attack at the beginning of the battle. She could see the damage he'd wrought: felled trees, slashed and chewed trunks, gigantic prints like trident runes. She felt a pang of remorse for having directed Sue to kill the lumbering beast. Stanley had only been following orders.

Much like she'd only been following Leo's.

"Where are we going?" Dot asked, not kindly.

"You'll see," was all Leo said before he went back to whistling.

Several minutes later they exited the forest and were welcomed by a lavish mansion on a hill. The house itself was an emerald green with white pillars at the front, as well as white shutters on the windows that looked functional instead of decorative. The place had to have twenty, maybe thirty rooms. It was huge, the kind of house owned by people who could afford to pay other people to clean up after them.

The entrance to the driveway was gated, but there was no guard in the shack, and the gate was open. After all, who needed security when they had a whole-ass dinosaur army at their beck and call?

"Whoa," Victoria said. "Nice digs."

"Fancy," Dot said, but there was no actual awe in her voice. She was focused more on Leo as the man trekked through the open gate and began walking up the hill.

"What's he doing?" Victoria asked.

"Oh, I have an idea. Come on."

They followed him up the winding drive, which was lined with bushes like billiard balls. It was not lost on Dot that the shrubbery, as well as the grass beyond it, was well groomed. Keeping a lawn this immaculate took time and effort, not to mention a shit load of water.

"That bitch really knew how to live, didn't she?" Leo asked as he bounced up the steps to the front door. "What are these stairs? Fuckin' marble, for fuck's sake?" He laughed, and once again, Dot and Victoria glanced at each other.

Something wasn't right here.

Leo threw the double doors open and stepped inside.

"Honey, I'm home!" he called, before devolving into giggles. This grown-ass man, this tough-as-nails military man, was actually, *legitimately* fucking *giggling*.

"Leo," Dot said, "what the fuck is going on here?"

Leo swung around and raised Crow's rifle. He smiled at them over the sights.

"What the hell, Leo?" Victoria hollered as she threw her hands into the air.

Dot, however, didn't move.

"She told you about the water, didn't she?" Leo said, still grinning even as he spoke. "The bitch told you I wanted the water. Tell me the truth now. Didn't she?"

Dot nodded but refused to break eye contact. The barrel of the rifle seemed larger than was possible. Its black maw opened wide before her, promising to gobble her up. What would it feel like to be shot point blank? Would she feel anything at all? Or would she slip painlessly into the void and return to the stardust from which she'd been created?

Victoria said, "What water? What the fuck are you two talking about?"

"Oh, shut the fuck up," Leo said. He swung the gun in Victoria's direction and pulled the trigger. Victoria spun away, hit the ground hard, and was still. Dot went for her, but Leo hollered, "Ah, ah, ah, you spoiled cunt. Stay where you are. I should kill you now, but I wanna know how these shoes work."

"Fuck you." Dot growled. Every ounce of her wanted to go to Victoria, to see if she was okay. They would make it through this, somehow. Dot just had to buy some time, keep Leo talking.

"If you don't wanna talk, I guess this is goodbye."

Dot's arms shot out in front of her. "Wait!"

"It's amazing how imminent death makes someone talkative. Spill it, bitch."

"She told me how the shoes work, but I'm not entirely sure if they'll work for you." Dot lied, but Leo didn't know that.

He glowered. "Tell me."

"They're psychically linked to the dinosaurs. You can control them. This can all end. You can all live in peace."

"Who the fuck cares about *peace*?"

"What?" Dot said, honestly puzzled.

"We're the ones who did this, kiddo. *We're* the ones who turned the dogs into dinosaurs, and the cats into apes. My team was working on a chemical we could drop on enemy nations that couldn't be detected. You know, Geneva Convention, and all that bullshit. They stumbled upon the concoction by accident. But our government, man, they didn't give a fuck about us. I'm the one who spearheaded the research! It was my fuckin' idea! And they fuckin' *canned me!*"

"You don't seem the scientific type," Dot said.

Leo growled at her.

"Just sayin'..."

"I was the team's commander. The scientists were my subordinates. Do you think CEOs of car manufacturers know how to work the assembly line?"

"Maybe? If they worked their way up and——"

"Shut up!" Leo shook his head, as if their conversation had stunned him. "The point is, I got fired, so I let the cat out of the bag. Or, should I say, *dog*?" He laughed at his own terrible joke.

"Are you saying you killed the world..." Dot said, "because you got fired?"

"*That job was all I had!*" Leo screamed. "The fuck would you know about working your ass off day and night only to be told you don't matter, that all your hard work was *unconscionable*? *Huh*? How would you feel? They said I was evil! The fuckin' nerve!"

"Hey, man," Dot said, "I'm gonna have to agree with them on that evil part."

Leo barked laughter before relaxing a bit. "You got a point. Anyway, I don't give a fuck about peace because it's never been about survival. It was about revenge. The water is just the icing on the cake, as it were. I need the water, of course, but I can't get to the water if I don't know how to use the shoes. I'd be torn apart hunting for the source. So, if you don't have the information I need, I'll just have to kill you and figure it out myself."

"Men can't use them," Dot lied.

"Come on, now, girl, I'm not fuckin' stupid. That bitch had an Adam's apple. You're gonna have to do better than that."

"Of course, *they* could use them," she said without hesitation. "They made them!"

Leo glared over the sights at her, unsure, but she could tell she was breaking through his defenses. He might not fully believe her yet, but the seeds of doubt had been planted. Now to further confuse him by changing the subject and buying them more time.

The Bitch had said that there was an artesian spring running underground all over this area. If that's what Leo wanted to know, she'd dangle the info in front of his face like a carrot for a horse.

"No shit? Makes sense, I guess," he said. For a moment, Dot had no idea what he was talking about, but then she realized he was responding to her claim that the Bitch could use the shoes because they'd invented them. "I guess we look for the water source together, eh? Another adventure, for old times' sake. Whataya say, girl?"

"Yeah, yeah, sure. Just one thing..."

"What's that?"

"This."

Dot kicked out her right leg, and the shoe sailed off her foot. It was enough of an unexpected distraction that Dot was able to close the few feet between she and Leo and tackle the man to the ground. She landed on top of him. Air kicked from his chest and he blew some of the nastiest breath Dot had smelled into her face.

"Do you not brush your teeth? Goddamn!" she yelled as she punched the man dead in the nose. Blood gushed. He tried to swing the gun up, but Dot grabbed his wrist and slammed his hand into the floor. His knuckles rapped the tile and he cried out in pain. The long-gun went clattering away.

"Get. *Off.* ME!" Leo roared. He brought up his knee, lightning quick, and caught her right between the legs. She had no balls to injure, but that didn't mean the force of the contact alone didn't hurt like hell. Grimacing through the pain, she punched him again. He'd been bringing his head up, so when her fist hit his nose this time, the impact drove the back of his skull into the tile. The *crack* was loud, sickening. His eyes swam in their sockets.

For the briefest instance, Dot thought she'd won. She thought she'd bested the fucking bastard. But then there was a loud *POP!* and something hot tore through her midsection. She reached down and felt blood pouring from her stomach. Leo's handgun went off again, and another round punched through her. She tumbled off him, if for no other reason than to stop him shooting her again. Not that he couldn't have rolled over and put a bullet in her head; he could have, but she wasn't thinking clearly at that moment.

"You gahdam *bish*!" Leo mumbled. His voice was thick and nasally, made so by his broken nose.

Where was the long-gun? Her bloody hand slapped around feebly trying to locate it. She'd rolled off him in the direction it had gone, but she couldn't find it. Wasn't that just her fucking luck? Here she was in strange world, and some psychopath with a shoe fetish had murdered her. Up until now, she'd survived being chased by a T-Rex, being dropped by a pterodactyl, and numerous other brushes with death, but this? *This* is what was going to kill her?

Oh, fuck off.

"I would've let you live if you'd just told me..." Leo said as he rolled onto his side and raised his handgun, the barrel aimed directly at Dot's head. "...how to use the fuggin' shoes."

Dot looked up and away from Leo. She didn't want to see her own death coming. Let him shoot her in the side of the head, for all she cared. Her stomach hurt like hell. She could feel it swelling with blood. No doubt she didn't have long; or maybe she did. Didn't it take a long time to die from a gunshot wound to the...?

"Oh," Dot said. "Hey, baby."

"Hey," Victoria said. She was standing about a foot away, Crow's AR-15 in her hands, aiming down at Leo. "I'll be with you just one second."

Dot closed her eyes as the glorious cacophony of the AR-15 blessed her ears.

§ § §

Victoria kept firing into Leo until the magazine ran dry. Then she beat his bloody face in with the stock of the rifle. Satisfied that Leo was good and dead—hell, how could he *not* be after all that?—she went to check on Dot.

Dot was in a bad way, there was no doubt about that. Victoria had to get her back to the park quick, but how?

She glanced around, as if something that might fly them away to safety would appear if she just searched hard enough.

And, holy shit, it did.

"Hang on, babe. I got you, I got you. Just hang on."

When Dot had tackled Leo, he'd dropped the witch's shoes. Victoria rushed over, slipped her feet inside of them, and, not knowing how else to use them, she willed as hard as she could for anything with wings in the general vicinity to come to the rescue. Then she went back to Dot. Dot was still breathing, albeit shallowly. Didn't it take a long fucking time to die of a gunshot wound to the stomach? Isn't that what every Western in existence taught you, that being gut-shot came with an extended and torturous death? But medicine had come a long way. They had treated gunshot wounds before––like when Foil shot himself in the foot, or when Larry got all sad and tried to blow his own fool head off but only ended up shooting through his cheek. Of course, neither of those instances were gut shots, but she had to hope. That was all she had left: hope.

Outside, a tremendous screeching caw sounded, a second before something big landed on the marble steps. The double doors were still open, so Victoria could see clearly the giant leathery bird-thing sitting on the steps, staring at her, as if asking, "You rang?"

"Come on, Dot. Calvary's here. Time to fly."

CHAPTER 20

The Lost Princess

Hunched over the desk in the witch's library, Victoria poured over an ancient tome, looking for the answer. It had to be there.

It.

Had.

To.

In a fugue state brought on by blood loss and a raging fever, Dot had talked about how she'd arrived in the park that fateful day, how she'd been transported there in the heart of a tornado. Whether it was the ramblings of a dying girl, or something more, Victoria didn't know.

Victoria *had* witnessed Dot drop out of the sky––in a dumpster of all damn things—so the tornado seemed to fit. How else could she have she gotten up there? And then there was Dot's confusion at finding the world overrun with dinosaurs. It had been years since Leo's bruised male ego had brought about the apocalypse. It didn't make sense that the tornado could have carried her around for years. For all kinds of reasons. Not the least of which was, Dot definitely would have mentioned being trapped in a dumpster for years.

That had led Victoria to the improbable truth: the tornado had somehow pulled Dot out of one world and deposited her into another.

Magic. Just like the witches' scaly slippers.

It was possible––again, however improbable––that the witches had conjured the tornado. Victoria had no idea why they'd used it to pluck Dot, of all people, from her world to fight Leo and not someone like, say, Arnold the-Fucking-Terminator Schwarzenegger. But it wasn't the *why* that mattered; it was the *how*. If she could find whatever spell they'd used to bring Dot here, maybe she could use it to escape this nightmare.

It had been two weeks, following the confrontation with the Bitch and Leo, since Victoria had moved into the siblings' mansion so she could devote her time to finding the answer. A couple of the other survivors from Homosapien Park stopped by every few days to drop off food, but Victoria wasn't all that interested in eating. Scouring the library and reading took up all of her time. It wasn't healthy, of that she'd been reminded regularly, but Victoria didn't care. For the first time in too many years, she'd found hope.

The library itself looked like something out of a movie. Bookshelves lined the ten-foot walls, each with books stacked to the ceiling and a sliding ladder on wheels. A large Victorian desk took up the center of the room––or maybe it was Renaissance. Who the fuck knew? Who the fuck cared? It was Jurassic, now.

On this particular morning, Victoria had come downstairs after a short nap, Tutu trailing behind her, and found a leather-bound grimoire with symbols of the four elements stamped on the cover. It looked promising. She'd spent the last two hours skimming the section labelled *Air*, but as she approached the last few pages, without even a hint of a teleporting-tornado spell in sight, that glimmer of hope began to fade. Tutu must have felt it too, because he'd lost interest and had fallen asleep with his head on her foot.

Closing one eye and squinting the other, she turned the last page.

"EUREKA!"

Tutu leaped to his feet. He gave a little turkeysaurus bark-squawk and started running in circles next to Victoria's chair.

"Babe, you're literally the only person on the planet who says *eureka* unironically."

Dot stood in the doorway of the library, leaning against the frame and smirking, as if she'd just gotten away with something nefarious.

Victoria collapsed into the chair, breathing heavily. She was exhausted.

"Although," Dot continued, "I guess that isn't really saying much, since most of the people on the planet are fuckin' corpses."

Victoria rolled her eyes. "Did I wake you?"

"Nah. Leo's parting gifts took care of that." Dot rubbed a hand over her stomach. "You know I can't sleep more than a few hours. Once the pain pills wear off, it's *No Sleep till Brooklyn*." She sang the last bit in her cute, but horrendously tone-deaf, singing voice. It made Victoria smile.

"Well, I think I found something." Victoria spun the giant book around and pushed it across the desk.

Dot hobbled over and, resting her hand on the tabletop, skimmed the pages laid out before her. Victoria got up and came around to help support her girlfriend's weight. After a moment, Dot glanced over and smiled.

"You did it," she said. "I can't fuckin' believe it. We're going home."

Tutu came around the corner of the desk and *yipped*, bouncing from foot to foot. Victoria chuckled under her breath. Then she leaned in, kissed Dot hard on the lips, and clicked her heels together three times.

THE END

ACKNOWLEDGEMENTS

It's pretty amazing to have so many people to thank on this, my first release. When I started on this crazy, solitary journey of turning my passion for words into a career, I wouldn't have imagined it. A couple close friends and family, maybe. Instead, I have a seemingly endless list of people to thank, many of whom I've only ever met in-person once, and some not at all. I guess that's the power of the Internet, the good it can do.

First, to Leslie, my partner and the mother of my children. In the six years we've been together, no one has shown me more support. From encouraging me to take this journey, to watching the kids so I could dedicate time to doing the work, to listening to me ramble about story ideas and other random writing shenanigans, I couldn't have done any of this without you.

To my children, Coleson and Samara. It wasn't so long ago that I was afraid I'd never get to meet either of you, and the road from there to here nearly broke me, several times. But I wouldn't change a thing. Everything I am, all of my experiences, brought me to you. I love you both more than you'll ever know and more than any words can describe.

My brothers, John Stevens and Kevin Watkins. We may have had three different sets of parents, but I couldn't have asked for more amazing siblings. You were both there when I started on this path, decades ago, reading endless drafts of stories (some better than others), providing feedback, and encouraging me to press on when imposter syndrome threatened to steal my drive. I wouldn't be here if not for you. And to Kevin specifically, your passing created a void that can never be filled. You will be on my mind and in heart as long as I draw breath.

I don't think I could list all the amazing writers I've befriended on Twitter the past few years, without missing some (apologies to anyone I may have missed). This lot of talented individuals has had a profound impact on me and my writing. They inspire me daily and have often provided a much need distraction from the perils of spending so much time in front of a computer screen, alone. In no particular order: Jonathan Janz, Jeremy Hepler, Cina Pelayo, Joshua Marsella, Kevin Whitten, Patrick McDonough, Brennan LaFaro, Lydian Faust, Michael Patrick Hicks, S.H. Cooper, Todd Keisling, Duncan Ralston, Michael Clark, Ian Bain, and Gabino Iglesias.

To John F.D. Taff, Samantha Kolesnik, Steve Stred, Sonora Taylor, TC Parker, Tracy Robinson, Sadie Hartmann, and Wilson Buck. This selfless group of people gave us their precious time by reading the book early on, providing invaluable feedback and edits and writing blurbs to help us get the word out on this crazy story. I appreciate every one of you.

I wouldn't have had the nerve to tackle this project if it weren't for Lee Murray. My mentor and friend, Lee took me under her wing and taught me so much in such a short period of time, transforming not only my writing but my self-confidence, as well. I could not have asked for a more amazing mentor.

To Laurel Hightower; it's all her fault, every bit of it. Laurel not only inspired this story and pushed Ward and I to write it, but she was also one of the first people to read it and even wrote the Forward. Past that, Laurel was the first writer on Twitter to befriend me and make me feel welcome in the Horror Writing Community. My sister in horror, thank you for everything you do.

Finally, to my collaborator and friend, Ward Nerdlo. When we started on Rex, we hardly knew each other and neither of us had read the other's work. Hell, I didn't even know Ward was an established writer with a catalogue of books that could rival Steven King's. And yet... and yet, he took a chance on me, someone who only had a handful of short story and poetry publications to his name. More importantly, he treated me like an equal, and for that I will forever be in his debt. It's been my absolute pleasure working with you, and I'm glad I'm now able to call you brother.

– Daron Kappauff,
October 19, 2021

§ § §

Hello, everybody. E. here. Or Edward Lorn. Or Ward Nerdlo. Or... well, the list goes on, doesn't it. I'll be brief, no worries.

I would like to thank Daron Kappauff, my brother and collaborator, for taking this insane journey with me. He came into my life at the perfect time, and was there for me during the worst moment of my existence: the death of my mother. Working with him was a joy from start to finish. We seem to share the same brain in a lot of ways, so challenging each other to top the last person's chapter was tremendous fun. We joke and say we threw each other under the bus, chapter after chapter, but the truth is that we figured out real quick that no matter what situation we put each other in, the other was gonna find a way out. You might think that pantsing a novel (we didn't plot a word of this book) with a stranger would be a headache, but when the other person seems to be an extension of yourself... well, what's that saying about doing what you love and never working a day in your life?

Yeah, *that*.

I won't bore you thanking all the same people Daron thanked, but I will extend my gratitude to everyone he listed. Thank you, one and all.

Now, excuse us, we have work to do.

Gremlins meets *I am Legend* sounds fun...

– Ward Nerdlo
November 30, 2021

ABOUT THE AUTHORS

DARON KAPPAUFF is a content editor by profession and a member of the Horror Writers Association (HWA). His work has appeared in numerous short fiction and poetry literary journals, he was a top five finalist in Crystal Lake Publishing's 2021 poetry contest, and his horror comic book, *Eternal Autumn*, was created and funded through Kickstarter. He lives in Missouri where he's raising a pair of toddlers and dabbles in conjuring the occult.

WARD NERDLO is the pseudonym of a pen name. Without his existence, jelly wouldn't set, fires would burn cold, and Christmas in July would be nothing more than mass speculation. He enjoys flights of fancy, burning toast, being confusing, and repurposing photos of friends for his own nefarious means.